Sophie Alexander

Sorel Kairé

Copyright 2021 by Sorel Kairé

All rights reserved

"Sophie Alexander" is a work of fiction. Names, characters, places and incidents are the product of the author's imagination or are used fictitiously. Any resemblance to actual events, locales or persons, living or dead, is coincidental.

The scanning, uploading, and distribution of this book without permission is a theft of the author's intellectual property. If you would like permission to use material from the book (other than for review purposes), please go to Website: sorelkaire.com

Thank you for your support of the author's rights.
First Edition: December 2021

Library of Congress Control Number: 1-10929003701

Cover Picture courtesy of Lex Passaris
Graphic Design by Soap Studio Inc.

ISBN: 978-1-7368653-1-6

Table of Contents

Prologue..................................1
Chapter One: Sophie......................5
Chapter Two: Sophie.....................10
Chapter Three: Sophie...................12
Chapter Four: Alex......................16
Chapter Five: Sophie....................19
Chapter Six: Sophie.....................24
Chapter Seven: Alex.....................29
Chapter Eight: Sophie...................34
Chapter Nine: Sophie....................36
Chapter Ten: Alex.......................38
Chapter Eleven: Sophie..................42
Chapter Twelve: Alex....................45
Chapter Thirteen: Alex..................48
Chapter Fourteen: Alex..................50
Chapter Fifteen: Sophie.................52
Chapter Sixteen: Alex...................58
Chapter Seventeen: Sophie...............61
Chapter Eighteen: Alex..................64
Chapter Nineteen: Sophie................66
Chapter Twenty: Alex....................68
Chapter Twenty-one: Sophie..............70
Chapter Twenty-two: Sophie..............72
Chapter Twenty-three: Alex..............74
Chapter Twenty-four: Sophie.............76
Chapter Twenty-five: Sophie.............82
Chapter Twenty-six: Sophie..............86
Chapter Twenty-seven: Alex..............87
Chapter Twenty-eight: Alex..............89
Chapter Twenty-nine: Sophie.............93
Chapter Thirty: Alex....................96
Chapter Thirty-one: Sophie.............103
Chapter Thirty-two: Alex...............106
Chapter Thirty-three: Sophie...........112
Chapter Thirty-four: Alex..............114
Chapter Thirty-five: Sophie............117
Chapter Thirty-six: Alex...............119
Chapter Thirty-seven: Sophie...........121
Chapter Thirty-eight: Lu and Olivia....123
Chapter Thirty-nine: Alex..............125
Chapter Forty: Alex....................128
Chapter Forty-one: Sophie..............129
Chapter Forty-two: Alex................134
Chapter Forty-three: Alex..............136
Chapter Forty-four: Alex...............140
Chapter Forty-five: Alex...............143
Chapter Forty-six: Sophie..............147
Chapter Forty-seven: Alex..............150
Chapter Forty-eight: Sophie............154
Chapter Forty-nine: Alex...............156
Chapter Fifty: Sophie..................159
Chapter Fifty-one: Alex................161
Chapter Fifty-two: Sophie..............163
Chapter Fifty-three: Alex..............167
Chapter Fifty-four: Sophie.............172
Chapter Fifty-five: Sophie.............175
Chapter Fifty-six: Alex................179
Chapter Fifty-seven: Sophie............186
Chapter Fifty-eight: Alex..............190
Chapter Fifty-nine: Sophie.............195
Chapter Sixty: Alex....................198
Chapter Sixty-one: Sophie..............200
Chapter Sixty-two: Sophie..............202
Chapter Sixty-three: Alex..............205

Chapter Sixty-four: Sophie..........209
Chapter Sixty-five: Alex..............210
Chapter Sixty-six: Alex...............213
Chapter Sixty-seven: Sophie.........214
Chapter Sixty-eight: Sophie.........217
Chapter Sixty-nine: Sophie..........220
Chapter Seventy: Alex.................222
Chapter Seventy-one: Sophie.......224
Chapter Seventy-two: Alex..........226
Chapter Seventy-three: Sophie.......227
Chapter Seventy-four: Alex..........229
Chapter Seventy-five: Sophie.......231
Chapter Seventy-six: Alex...........234
Chapter Seventy-seven: Sophie.....237
Chapter Seventy-eight: Sophie.......245
Chapter Seventy-nine: Alex..........248

Chapter Eighty: Sophie..............253
Chapter Eighty-one: Alex............257
Chapter Eighty-two: Sophie.........260
Chapter Eighty-three: Alex...........263
Chapter Eighty-four: Sophie.........266
Chapter Eighty-five: Sophie.........267
Chapter Eighty-six: Alex.............269
Chapter Eighty-seven: Sophie.......271
Chapter Eighty-eight: Alex..........274
Chapter Eighty-nine: Sophie........276
Chapter Ninety: Alex....................282
Chapter Ninety-one: Sophie.........284
Chapter Ninety-two: Alex..............286
Epilogue: Sophie.......................289
Epilogue: Alex..........................290
Acknowledgements...................293

For all the Alex's out there
looking for their Sophie

And for you, Lu

A new beginning
To fill her soul
A place
Where she can be whole

Prologue

She moved with ease, grace and a desire to find a place, a life, a home. An adventure. She'd come into some money that afforded her the freedom to leave her familiar world behind. A world of sacrifice, endless hours of work in a good, caring environment, most of the time, but relentless, exhausting all the same. No spring chicken, she'd almost reached her sixth decade. A memorable milestone in a life well lived. She prided herself in her work ethic, her loving nature, her enthusiasm. She was loved, yet she did not have the love she'd longed for her whole life. She thought about her parents sometimes, both long gone. An only child, pampered, spoiled. Cherished. Her mother used to tell stories of her childhood. One in particular danced around her mind more often than not. It seemed one autumn day on their way to the pumpkin patch, dressed as a turkey, aching to carve a few pumpkins, she confided to her mother she was in love. Her mother swallowed a laugh, said, "Honey, what do you know of love? You're only eleven."

"I know, Mama," she'd responded. "It's just life is so sad without a love." And sad it had been. Well, not really sad, she'd loved, been loved, but never the burning passion her eleven-year old self wished for. Never 'the' love.

Surrounded by affection, she'd walked through life. Radiated the sweetest most giving energy. People flocked to her side, wanted some of that warmth to rub off on them. Generous with her light, sometimes she needed to hibernate in order to re-charge her batteries. Found refuge in sleep, in quiet, in books, in the early hours of the morning, her favorite time. That moment of darkness before the day was born brought comfort to her heart. She'd get out of bed, fire up the Nespresso machine, make herself a sweet milky concoction with two very strong, smooth shots of espresso. Sometimes she dunked a cookie in her cup, closed her eyes, savored the flavor of love. Food was love to her. She rejoiced, reveled in it. Filled the hole in her heart that wished for the elusive romance. It's not that she did not feel complete. She was complete, whole.

She just longed for 'the one' to dance into her life. To dance with her.

She was shy though she would never be perceived as shy. Open, inviting. With everyone. Except, she was. Shy. Kept her heart hidden, shielded. Beautiful in an unusual way. Her light, her eyes, her soul sparkled bright, enchanting. Her body was not of this time. She had a little 'extra.' She joked, "more surface to love," "look at all this deliciousness," she'd say, mocking herself. Her motto, *I'll say it first so you won't hurt me.* Baffled her when people said she'd gained weight, as if she didn't know. As if she didn't live with herself every day of her life. As if she didn't try to eat a little less, move a little more. The unfulfilled yearning would rear its ugly head only to be assuaged by ice cream, the dopamine for the heart, the soul.

Love, she thought. That ship sailed a long time ago. In a few months, well, eleven and a half to be exact, she would turn sixty. Nobody over the age of sixty ever found the love she longed for. Made her sad. Another one of her mottos, she had many, *there is no expiration date on a dream.* But was there? On this one? Maybe. If she could wish for something it'd be a younger, fearless version of herself with courage in her heart. Courage to leap with faith and wonder, courage to believe love was possible, for her. Courage to love... to love a man in the romantic all-engulfing meaning of giving herself wholly to someone. Without fear. Without reservation. But it was too late

now. Her dream had expired. But maybe there was another dream.
    So she wished for something different.

Chapter One

Sophie

Sophie's phone woke her from a deep sleep.

"Hello," she answered. Seven on the dot. Dang, she'd overslept.

"Sophie Alexander, please," a man's voice on the other end of the line.

"This is Sophie," rubbed her eyes awake.

"Jordan Walters here. I represent the estate of Douglas Fairbanks."

"I'm sorry. You must have the wrong person."

"You are Sophie Alexander, head of human resources at The Shoe Company in Portland, right?"

"That's me."

"Then you're the Sophie I'm looking for."

"I don't know a Mr. Fairbanks."

"I'm aware, however, he knew you very well."

"I-he-what?"

"Mr. Fairbanks passed away last month and left you something in his will."

"Oh, I'm sorry, but I really have no clue who he is."

"I know. Like I said, you wouldn't know him by name. You may not even remember him, but he never forgot you."

"What do you mean?"

"I think you better come to my office and I'll explain. You're in Portland, right?"

"Yes."

"Come to my office next Monday at five-thirty. Does that work for you?"

"Sure."

Sophie walked out of Mr. Walters' office at seven twenty-three p.m., manila envelope in hand. Headed north to meet Annie for dinner. Annie knew everything about Sophie since they were eight. Two left feet each, an unrelenting, mean prima ballerina discouraged both of them from following their shared dream of dancing Clara in The Nutcracker, of dancing anything in anything. Two peas in a pod, inseparable, their lives went in opposite directions, but their connection stayed the same. Annie had grandchildren, a loving husband, a house. Sophie had a job, a condo, a king-sized bed all to herself, because, why not? The promise of a man sharing it one day loomed large, that is until she turned sixty.

Annie knew about the meeting with the lawyer. They'd goggled Douglas Fairbanks over a glass of wine, or three, the Saturday before. Found the actor, then the man. Sophie's Fairbanks looked oddly familiar.

"I think I know him," Sophie said. "Can't place him, though."

"An old lover, and by that I mean old."

"Stop it! The man is dead."

"Precisely. You've had some wild times, Alexander, wild."

"Annie, focus."

"You focus. I'm drinking. John is in such trouble tonight. I want him."

"Go you sex fiend, go ravage your husband."

Annie was Sophie's anchor, the voice of reason when Sophie needed direction, comfort. She quickened her pace, eager to get to the restaurant, share the news with her friend.

"So?" Annie asked. Sophie dropped the envelope in front of Annie, took the seat next to her. The restaurant was hopping, loud, fun, brimming with young people making connections.

Annie opened the envelope, read.

"Sophie, what the hell? The man left you a cottage by the sea. That's your dream, Sophe, and he left you money."

"I-I'm just overwhelmed by all of this."

"Why did he do it?"

Sophie pulled a letter from the pile, handed it to Annie. Annie read it out loud.

"Dear Sophie,

I bet you don't know who I am, but I know who you are. Never forgot your kindness, the way you reached out to a complete stranger, eased his pain with a simple smile, a hello, a hug. You made a difference in my life all those years ago and I want to make a difference in yours. I thought about reaching out to you so many times, telling you how you saved me that day, how you gave me hope, a hope I thought was forever gone. But I didn't. You had your life. I kept up with you though, knew if you ever needed anything, I would be there for you, but you never needed me.

Giving you a gift, small in comparison to what you gave me, to make your life easier, like you did mine. This home brought light into my life, the light you saw in a heart that had dimmed. Your kindness gave me hope. I gift you a view, a home, a little freedom. A new beginning. Always room for a new beginning, right Sophie? Thank you, Sophie Alexander. Thank you. May the rest of your life be as lovely as you.

Yours,

Douglas Fairbanks."

Annie dropped the paper, looked up at Sophie's face.

"Hey, hey, Sophe, don't cry. This is beautiful," Annie said.

"I think I remember him. But it was too many years ago, you know, just a man who was clearly heartbroken." Sophie shrugged, wiped a tear with the back of her hand.

"So what happens now?" Annie asked.

"I don't know. It's just a bit overwhelming."

Annie placed her hand over Sophie's. Squeezed.

The waitress approached, asked what they wanted to eat. Sophie's face softened, the sadness eased a little.

"Hmm, I'll start with the Caprese salad, then pasta Bolognese, please. Al dente. And a bottle of Prosecco," Sophie said.

"Make that two."

"No, Annie, you have to get something different, so we can share."

"As if I didn't know you, Alexander," Annie laughed. "I'll have the Caesar's salad, chicken piccata, lots of garlic bread please. And only one bottle of Prosecco Rosé."

Chapter Two

Sophie

Took two months to get her affairs in order. Rented out her condo. Gave notice, trained the new head of personnel, packed up her life, headed to the beach. She'd seen the cottage. Love at first sight. A row of houses lined the Oregon coast, wood, porches facing the ocean, patch of grass, gardens. Heaven. Her cottage, wow, her cottage, her dream come true, painted a soft yellow, window trims blue. Big. Twice the size of her two bedroom, one den apartment back in Portland. The cottage had three bedrooms. Huge walk-in closet, every woman's dream, master bathroom with freestanding tub, separate shower. Needed work, she'd have to glam it up. A little too masculine now, but give her time and it'd be perfect. Three bathrooms, a big space on the second floor for an office/art room. Sophie had always wanted an art room. For her jewelry, her painting. And the kitchen, oh the kitchen. Joy. State of the art. Huge. Sophie loved to cook. Filled the part of her heart that had a little hole in it, that needed comfort. Light, light, light everywhere. And the view, it took her breath away. A large porch faced the water, just like she'd always dreamed. Haystack Rock visible in the distance, sand, water, sky. Fresh air. Fueled her soul. Wow! All in all, perfect place to start the third act of her life. Sixty, nine and a half months away and counting, but who was counting?

Car packed, smile on her face, Sophie hugged Annie good-bye, drove the hour and a half to her new life.

Chapter Three

Sophie

There he was, on a step ladder, fixing the light on the front porch of the cottage next door. Rippled back. Long, lean, strong legs. Perfect ass. Sophie loved a good ass on a man. Arms that made her want to be held in them. Yes, there he was, the most gorgeous young creature she'd ever seen. Had she said young? Had she said gorgeous? Had she said creature? Yep, she had. Took a step up, cleared her throat.

He turned. Not as young as she thought but his face took her breath away. She found his eyes. Ah, the eyes. Eyes which reflected anger, lightness, beauty, kindness, love, hurt, all in one fell swoop. But now, as they looked at her, they were annoyed. Sophie blushed a little, certain that women all over swooned under his dark gaze, the contour of his perfect chiseled chin. Geez, she'd have to stop reading romance novels, but... his nose, a bit too big, his lips, a little too full, but all together, his face, perfect harmony. There she went again, letting her corny literary choices paint her thoughts. She dared not look at the size of his feet, his hands. Knees weakened faced with so much beauty. Yes, he was beautiful, so way out of her chubby league. Together they'd make a perfect ten. He, the one. She, the zero. Fitting metaphor of what would never be, but a girl could dream, right? Nope. Not this girl. Not anymore.

"What?" he barked.

Charming, she thought. "Hey, sorry, didn't mean to startle you. I'm Sophie. New next door neighbor."

He squinted, took her in.

"Just moved into Mr. Fairbanks' cottage. Older woman here. Not very handy, in fact, not handy at all. Two left hands," Sophie waved her hands in front of his face, nervous talking. "Having a bit of trouble figuring out the fireplace among other things. Any chance you're the handyman in the neighborhood, as you are so clearly fixing my neighbor's light, and I could hire you to give me a hand with a few things?"

Sophie smiled, pushed the attraction she felt for this man way out of her head, her body. Yep, her body reacted to his scent, fresh, citrusy, tinted with sweat. Nope. *Shut it down, now Sophie,* she thought. Now. That part of her life, over. All she would get now would be an old geezer who needed a nurse, a companion, because all healthy geezers wanted a twenty-five year old babe on their arm. She was no babe. She helped Cinderella to the ball, not the other way around.

"I'm your neighbor," he said, annoyance in his voice.

"Oh, right, sorry," she said.

He looked at her, said nothing.

"No worries then. As you were." she said, did an about face, thankful at his unfriendly tone. Better to keep her away from him. No need to engage in a friendship.

"Wait," he said. "Sorry. You took me by surprise."

"No worries."

"You said that already," irritation in his voice.

"So I did." *Jerk*, she thought, smile fake on her face. Frost covered her heart. *Not so handsome anymore*, she thought. Rude. Reminded her of a certain manager at work who was gorgeous until he opened his mouth. How quickly handsome uglies up with an unkind heart. She turned on her heel, double-stepped it back to her cottage, determined to never cross his path again. Rushed to her place. Her place. Thank you Mr. Douglas Fairbanks for gifting her freedom. And a second chance.

She heard a curse word behind her, footsteps followed hers.

"Hey, wait."

She didn't. Doubled her pace, took the steps up her porch two at a time, surprised she could still do that, slammed the kitchen door behind her. Sophie went straight to the freezer, chocolate peanut butter ice cream welcomed her home. Yes, it was cold. Yes, the fireplace needed help before she could light it. And a triple yes to ice cream, a girl's best friend.

Chapter Four

Alex

He stopped when he heard the 'click' of the lock punctuating her escape. The lady could run. What the hell? He was in a lousy mood. Seemed he was always in a mood these days. His new neighbor hadn't deserved his behavior, but he'd had it with women wanting things from him. Things he couldn't give. Wouldn't. He'd made a vow to never share his heart again. Alex shook his head. It'd been eleven years, four months, twelve days. Mattie had been his life. He'd had plenty of sex since then, never wanting for a warm female body to assuage his desire, his carnal desire, but women always wanted more. To catch him. He'd be damned if he'd get caught. Last night all he'd wanted was a beer or two, a plate of fish and chips, a chat with Liam, the owner of the Pub and his best friend, but Peggy knew he was around, hounded him until he took her home. She'd gotten too clingy so he'd broken up with her. She'd cried. Begged. Told him she loved him, said she'd make him love her. Made him angry. He'd been straight when they'd hooked up a few weeks before. A hook-up, that's all it was. He'd told her. Peggy agreed, eager in the notion that she'd change him. That he'd love her. Women always thought they'd change him. He was a grown man. Fifty-three for fuck's sake. Didn't they know? When a man tells his truth a woman should believe him. He didn't play games. Was not looking for commitment or love. No. But he'd been weak, his body needed relief, he'd caved last night. Now Peggy had called three times. Wanted to cook him dinner. He didn't want dinner with Peggy. Not today. Not ever.

"Shit," Alex said. Walters was going to kill him. He'd told him about Fairbanks' will, the new neighbor. Alex promised to be nice, helpful even. Fairbanks spoke of the mysterious woman who showed him the world could be kind, sweet, good. Saved him. He'd kept an eye on her all these years, waiting, knowing that if she ever needed anything, ever got in trouble, he'd be there. Like she'd done for him. He'd give her anything and everything she needed. But she'd managed without him. She worked hard, people loved her. Adored her. Douglas knew. He missed Douglas. Always the voice of reason. Never bullshit, always truth. But he was gone now, like his Mattie. God, he was pathetic. He'd been in a shit mood, Sophie had been the one to get the brunt of it. She hadn't deserved his rudeness. If Douglas were alive he'd be pissed.

Sophie, he thought. He'd felt something when he heard her voice. He'd been looking forward to meeting her but when he looked in her eyes, hazel, speckled with green and gold, something cracked. Beautiful eyes. Eyes that said everything, moved him. Pissed him off even more. He'd never be ready. Flings, hook-ups, the shorter the better, yes. Emotions. Hard no.

Chapter Five

Sophie

Sophie loved stretching, bending, feeling her muscles get more pliable by the second. Yoga. She remembered the first time she took a class. Fifty and fabulous but in terrible shape. "Ready to change?" Annie had said. She'd gotten a groupon for her birthday. Twenty classes. "Time to get healthy," Annie had said. Was it? Maybe? No, yes, it had been time. Anything to help her body stay young, age gracefully. She remembered how a little voice whispered *thank you* when the simple effort of keeping her arms straight, knees bent, Warrior Pose, sent a waterfall of sweat down her back. *Thank you*, screamed her body. She was hooked.

She'd been at the cottage almost a week, absolutely loved it. Her cottage. Reminded her of an English novel, minus the cliffs overlooking the stormy sea. Fit her like a glove. Fully unpacked. Everything in its place. She'd taken a walk the day before. Trees, flowers, quaint houses around her, smell of the ocean soothed her senses. Friendly neighbors waved hello. Nice. Main Street dotted with shops, cafes, and a small yoga studio five blocks from her new home. *Home*, she'd thought, heart warmed. Took a schedule, spotted 'an easy does it' class. Yoga, for her, was not about the difficulty of the class, it was about her soul, her sanity, her joints, her strength. No competition. So, mat in place, Sophie found herself in the corner of the room, women of all ages, a straggling man or two, blocks, straps, towels, blankets, all necessary for the hour and a half of stretching, bending, balance. Ah, balance, the true challenge for her. She used to joke balance was a metaphor for her life. A life out of balance. She had her mind set to bring it into balance.

"Ciao," a woman said, dropped her mat next to Sophie. "You're new."

Sophie looked up, found herself staring at a gorgeous, ageless woman. Exotic. Lean. Elegant. Dressed in expensive yoga attire. Sparkling diamonds in her ears. Enormous solitaire on her right hand.

"Hi," Sophie said. "Yes. Just moved here. My very first class."

"I'm Lu."

"Sophie."

The teacher walked in, greeted every student with a hello hug, a short conversation.

"You're going to love Olivia. Wise for such a young one. Amazing and sweet."

The instructor, a woman in her mid-twenties, stunning, walked up to Lu, hugged her, then turned her attention to Sophie.

"Hi. I'm Olivia," she said.

"Sophie."

"Welcome to class, Sophie. Have you practiced yoga before?"

"Yes."

"Anything I should be aware of? Problems?"

"Aside from old bones, a little extra padding, all good."

"Perfect."

Olivia finished her rounds of hello, took her place at the front of the class.

An hour and a half later, Sophie felt relaxed, oddly tired. She hadn't yoga'd in over three weeks. Knew her muscles would scream at her tomorrow.

"Favorite part of yoga class?" Lu gathered her mat.

"Savasana," Sophie replied.

"Girl after my own dreams. How about an espresso to pump us up, then a little shopping? Love to show you around."

"Latte?"

"Dairy free."

"Lactose intolerant?"

"How did you ever guess?"

"Psychic," Sophie winked.

"Don't wink, cara. Wrinkles."

"Italian?"

"How did you ever guess?"

"Psychic."

Lu let out a laugh, hugged Sophie. "I like you," she said. "Oooh, soft. Men must go wild over your softness, curves and delicious boobs. Tell me," she linked her arm in Sophie's, guided her out of the room. "About your lovers."

"How do you know I'm not married?"

"Oh, darling, it's written all over your face."

Sophie could not help but be charmed by Lu. So open. So strong. So beautiful. So fun. She was going to like it here.

"Come on. Espresso, then shopping. These sweats," pointed at Sophie's outfit. "Have got to go. We need to accentuate the waist I know is underneath all this flannel." Lu said.

Sophie's heart jumped. She'd just moved to a town by the water no less. Her dream. She didn't need to work anymore. The rent of her condo, her savings, the money Mr. Fairbanks left her, would keep her for a long time, while she figured out what she would do with the rest of her life. Maybe she'd finally give her jewelry making a go. She'd been doing it for years, all in her closet, afraid to sell. Maybe it was time. Maybe. Her life, different now. No longer in Portland. Annie had been happy for her. Annie and John were her family, her anchor. And now Lu, a woman so different from her on the outside, yet she felt the connection, the familiarity. Kindred.

"Lead the way, Lu. Latte awaits. And maybe a little pastry?"

Lu shot her a look. Horrified.

"What? You don't get this delicious without the help of a little somethin' somethin'... delicious," Sophie said.

"I like you," Lu laughed.

She'd said that already, Sophie thought, delighted. She'd made a friend.

Chapter Six

Sophie

Lu and Sophie sat at a table by the window overlooking the street. They ordered an espresso, a vanilla latte, a couple of almond croissants, a plate of fruit. "To be good," Lu told the waitress.

"So Sophie, what do you think of our little town?"

"I love it. I don't know, the moment I drove through, I felt something in my heart. Home."

"Hmmm," Lu said, "I get that."

"How long have you been here?"

"Four years. My third husband brought me on our honeymoon. When he died, I knew this was the place for me."

"Oh, I'm sorry."

"Don't be. We had a beautiful marriage. All three of my marriages were special."

"The other two?"

"Dead."

"Oh." Sophie could not even imagine the pain of losing one person you loved, let alone three. She reached her hand, placed it over Lu's, squeezed, sending as much loving energy as possible.

"Thank you," Lu said. "But I've been lucky. I've loved, really loved, three times in this life. Not many people are lucky. Not you."

Wow. It's as if Lu could see in her soul. "How?" Sophie asked.

"Psychic," Lu winked.

Sophie laughed out loud.

"I can feel it, Sophie," Lu continued. "You've not found him, or should I say he has not found you. Yet."

"No yet about it. That part of my life is over. For good."

"Oh, I don't think so."

"How can you say that?"

"It's a feeling," Lu said. Sophie's eyes filled. Was she that transparent? If Lu could tell how it made her sad not to have found love, could everyone see it? Shook her head. New beginning, right? Leaving the pathetic sadness behind. So what if sex was out of the equation? She had Bob, her battery operated boyfriend. He'd do. He would.

"Darling, sex is never out of the equation. And yes, you said it out loud."

What the heck?

"What the heck?" Lu echoed.

"Again?"

"Yes."

Laughter erupted between them. Easy. Fun.

"So, about your husbands," Sophie said a few minutes after the laughter died down. Lu turned her shoulder in Sophie's direction, pulled down her sweater, exposed a tattoo of a martini glass, three olives and droplets of liquid spilling into red lips. The hint of a scar lined her back, under the ink.

"An olive for each one of them. My love for them is imprinted on my skin."

"It's so beautiful and romantic," Sophie said, followed the droplets over the scar down Lu's back. "I've always wanted a tattoo."

"And?"

"Never got around to it."

"Well, we're just going to have to do something about that. Taking you to Benjamin. Oh, Ben. British Ben. Amazing Ben. Big Ben," Lu gave Sophie a knowing look. "Sex is never out of the equation."

Sophie's eyes widened, she giggled.

"Oh Lu, you have many stories to tell. I think I'll live vicariously through you."

"Why do that when you can live... vicariously."

Sophie laughed.

"Just sayin'," Lu said.

"Noted."

"So, where are you staying?"

"Funny thing, I inherited a cottage."

"Douglas' place. Oh, of course, you're her. Should have known the minute I saw your face. He talked about you sometimes, you know. How a smile, a word can change someone's world. You changed his."

"So I've been told. Funny, I sort of remember him, but it was so long ago. I don't even remember what I said."

"He never forgot."

Olivia, who had just ordered a chai tea, spotted them, walked up to their table.

"Sophie, how was class? Okay for you?"

"Just what I needed today. Now tomorrow I may not be able to move, but right now I feel good."

"Then come back tomorrow."

"Yes. We'll both be back. I have a yoga partner," Lu beamed.

"Good. May I join you? Waiting for my father. He's late."

"Of course. Sit," Sophie said.

"Olivia, Sophie here is your father's new neighbor," Lu said.

Olivia pulled a chair, sat.

"Okay then I need to apologize for Alex."

"Alex?"

"My father. Your neighbor. The jerk that growled at you."

"He's your father? Wait, how did you know?"

"He told me. I was impressed you slammed the door in his face. He's been too proud to apologize."

"Hello daughter, Lu, neighbor," a masculine voice piped up behind Sophie.

Sophie felt a tingle down her spine. The man had a voice like velvet, like sex. Voices did something to her. This one definitely did.

"Not too proud to apologize, just working up my courage to do so. You can be quite scary."

"You sure have a way with words, especially with apologies," Sophie said.

"I like her, Alex. Apologize!" Olivia said.

"Can we please start again? I'm Alex Carter, your dork of a neighbor who would be more than happy to take a look at a certain fireplace that seems to be giving you trouble. And who is very very sorry for being such a —"

"Jerk," Olivia said.

"Fool," Lu said.

"Yeah, what they said," Alex said.

Sophie smiled. "Well, how can I say no to my neighbor slash handyman offering to get my fireplace working again."

Olivia and Lu cracked up. Sophie blushed.

"Well, that's an offer I may not be able to refuse," Alex winked.

Chapter Seven

Alex

The next afternoon Sophie opened her kitchen door, Alex stood outside, toolbox in hand.

"Hello neighbor. Ready?" he asked.

"Come in," Sophie said. "Thank you, Alex."

She had a voice. Sweet, velvet, sexy. And those eyes. Again with the twinkling eyes.

"Lead the way, ma'am."

"Ma'am? Really? Young man, one thing we older ladies hate, capital letters HATE, is being called ma'am."

Sassy. He liked that. Older? No. She was not old. He pegged her for maybe, what? Fifty-four? Fifty-five at the most.

"Sorry. Sophie?"

"Better."

That mouth brought desire to the surface. What the hell? Thoughts pushed away. Not going there. Nope.

"By the way, we fifty-three year olds like it when you call us young."

"Hmmm," she smiled. "C'mon then, child, the fireplace awaits."

"Lead the way."

He smiled at her. Almost said something. He wanted to know how old she was. What she thought about. What she liked. She turned, walked ahead of him. He took in her shape. Curvaceous. Strong. Wow. Straight to his groin. Looked down, forced his body to settle. He had a fireplace to fix.

An hour later, he walked out of her cottage, found Sophie seated on the back porch, looking straight at the water, cup of tea in hand.

"Done," he showed her his hands. "And I didn't even get dirty."

"Thank you, Alex. Can I get you something to drink? Coffee? Tea? Wine?"

It was close to five.

"Wine," he said.

"Red or white?"

"Red please. Will you join me?"

"I will. Sit. Be right back."

Alex put his toolbox down. The porch, so different now. Her touches softened it. Flowers. Chairs with sky blue plush cushions. Soft, like her. He took the seat next to hers, looked out to the water. What a view. He never sat outside anymore. The vista from his porch was exactly the same, yet he hadn't enjoyed it in a very long time. He'd been hiding, punishing himself, not allowing anything good in his life.

Sophie returned with a bottle of red, a glass for Alex, a flute of what appeared to be pink champagne for her. She set them down on the coffee table, started to walk back into the cottage. He looked at her.

"Snacks."

A moment later she appeared with a tray of cheese, cold cuts, kalamata olives, slices of French bread, nuts, dates, green grapes.

"So Miss Sophie Alexander, what's your story?"

Sophie smiled, settled on her chair, took a sip of her Prosecco.

"I'm starting a new one. Here."

Best place to do that, he thought.

"Hmmm," he said, somehow comfortable in a little bit of silence. The sun was still strong, but soon the blue sky would turn all sorts of colors. He was ready for the show.

"No story before here then?" Alex asked after a quiet moment.

"Yes. A story. We all have one, right? What's yours Alex? Aside from you being fifty-three years old, having an amazing, gorgeous daughter, living next door to me, being a bit of a grouch sometimes, I know nothing about you."

"Hmmm," he said again.

"Tell me."

"What do you want to know?"

"What are you doing here, in this small town? You from here?"

"No. Moved with Olivia after her mother died." Straight to the point. The wound. The pain.

"Oh, I'm so sorry. I had no idea."

"It's okay. It was a long time ago."

"How long is a long time ago?" Sophie whispered.

"Eleven years, four months, nineteen days."

"Oh," she said. "I see."

"What do you see, Sophie Alexander?"

"That you miss her."

"Everyday."

"What's her name?"

Alex noticed Sophie didn't ask what her name was, no past tense. He liked that. He felt in that small word that she understood.

"Mattie."

"May I ask what happened? I mean, you don't have to talk about it if you don't want to."

"Cancer. She went fast. For that I'm grateful. She didn't suffer. Too much."

Alex felt the warmth of her hand on his. Sophie stayed quiet.

Chapter Eight

Sophie

Sophie sensed the sadness on his skin. Here a wound still open, oozed pain. Wow. What a love they must have shared if after eleven years, four months, nineteen days he felt as if it was only yesterday. That she knew. He counted the days. She said nothing, her hand on his.

"Thank you," he said after a few minutes, did not move his hand.

"Thank you?" she asked.

"For understanding."

"Ah. You're welcome."

Another moment or two of silence.

"So, my turn," Alex said. "Tell me something I don't know about you."

"That's easy. You don't know anything about me except that I'm your neighbor and can't fix a fireplace. Oh, and I like yoga."

"So tell me then. Something I don't know."

"I'm going to be sixty years old in less than ten months."

He turned to look at her. "I don't believe that for a second."

"It's true."

"No."

"Yes. I'm your elder, so believe it young one."

He laughed.

"Hey, show the old lady some respect," she said, removed her hand from his, had a sip of bubbly.

"Old lady my ass! You're one sassy woman," he said. "Really? Fifty-nine? I could have sworn you were around my age."

"What about my hair?"

"What about it?"

"It's white."

"I thought you were a platinum blonde. Like Marilyn Monroe."

"Alex Carter, changing my mind about you. I think I like you."

"I think I like you, too."

Chapter Nine

Sophie

"Who are you, Douglas Fairbanks? What led you to leave me, me, the hope of a better future? How did you know this was my dream? Well, one of my dreams, the one that hasn't expired. How could you know and why didn't you warn me a hunk of a grouchy man would be my neighbor?" Sophie knelt in front of a grave, arranged pink, yellow, purple, white wildflowers in a vase, wondered about the man that rested six feet under, her guardian angel. "Are you my fairy godfather? See, I think you are. Gifted me the chance to lust for... life," she cracked herself up. "Annie would be lifting her left eyebrow right about now. Oh, Douglas Fairbanks, thank you."

"Well hello there?"

Sophie looked up, took in a ragged breath, placed her right hand over her heart. "You scared me half-to death. For a second, I thought Mr. Fairbanks was speaking to me from the grave."

Alex chuckled. "Speak to the dead much?"

"Ah, well, not usually, but yes, I guess in this case I'm going to have to say yes. I-I know next to nothing about him. He seemed to know so much about me."

"What do you want to know?" Alex said, soft.

"Really?"

"I knew the man."

Chapter Ten

Alex

He did know Douglas. Well. Fairbanks sold him his cottage, took him under his wing when Olivia and Alex showed up, shell-shocked after Mattie's death. Fairbanks had been friends with his grandfather. Fairbanks was like a grandfather to him. To Olivia. He knew all about loss. Just like Alex.

He missed Douglas. Missed him like hell. Visited his grave whenever he needed to talk, just like he'd called on the cottage next door. Often. Her cottage now.

"Pretty flowers," Alex said, nodded towards the bouquet of wild flowers.

"Aren't they? They make me happy. Hope they'll make Douglas happy."

Douglas, Alex thought, *he loved his flowers.* Planted new ones every spring. Alex helped. He loved spending time with Douglas. Reveled in his stories, especially when he talked about Sophie. Sophie intrigued him. Soft on the outside. Was the inside equally as soft?

"What's your favorite flower?" Alex asked.

"Do I have to pick just one? There are so many beautiful ones, so many personalities, so many moods."

"Okay then, your least favorite one."

"Hmm..." Sophie pondered for a moment. "If I have to pick one, I'd say... the red rose."

"Red roses? Your least favorite?" That surprised him. Women loved red roses, long stemmed red roses, the longer the stem the more they loved them.

"Hmm-hmm."

"Why? The ever popular red rose, symbol of true love on Valentine's day, beloved by all, except apparently one Sophie Alexander, lover of wild flowers."

"It's not like that. I mean, the red rose is absolutely lovely, except it's the most unsurprising, uninteresting flower to me. If I were to pick a rose, it would be the orange one, full of fire, excitement."

"Orange roses, okay, noted. What else?"

"I love tulips."

"Any color?"

"Yes. They are badass, rebellious. Even wilted they are beautiful. And you? Favorite flower?"

Alex thought for a moment. A small smile curved his lips.

"I like the iris," he said, quiet.

"The independent flower."

"Independent?"

"Yes. Tall, lean, solitary but not lonely. The Audrey Hepburn of flowers."

The Audrey Hepburn of flowers? Okay.

"Alex," she said, soft.

He looked at her.

"Tell me about him," she said.

"Here?"

"Yes," she sat crossed-legged, comfortable, fiddled with the flowers. "I feel close to him here."

"So do I," Alex said. "I feel close to him in your cottage, too."

"Even with all the changes I've made?"

"Especially because of them. Douglas would speak about how he pictured your place in Portland would be. 'A home,' he'd say. 'Matches her soul.' He imagined you would soften anywhere you lived, anywhere you worked, anyone you touched. Exactly how you softened him."

"Yeah, about that, how did I do that?"

"Gently," he said.

She looked at him, confused. He kept his eyes on hers for a long while. She held his gaze.

"Did he have family?" Sophie managed to ask, dragging her eyes away from his.

"No." And yes. Alex and Olivia were his family. His chosen family.

"Was he ever married?"

"Yes," he played with the grass, pulled, pushed, pulled again.

"Do you not want to talk about this? It's okay if you don't want to," her voice gentle, depicting a touch of concern for him, like she could see in his heart. The crease in her brow told him she worried about his feelings, about the loss of his friend. His mentor. "I know he's important to you."

Alex missed him but knew things were the way they were supposed to be. Douglas had been in pain. Lots of pain. Physical pain. His passing brought relief. Relief of the pain for Douglas, relief of watching his friend suffer for him.

"No, it's okay. Time she got to know you, old man," he said to the tombstone before him.

Chapter Eleven

Sophie

"I have a very vague memory of him," she said. "What do you remember?"

"Nothing much, it's terrible. Just maybe he was slumping on a table outside a café. It was early. I could feel the sadness. Sometimes I can feel people's sadness."

Alex cleared his throat, pulled a piece of grass from the ground, moved it around his fingers, played with it.

"You hugged Douglas that day. He cried in your arms. You stroked his back, told him everything was going to be okay. Offered him a cup of tea."

"When I came out of the café he was gone."

"See, he wasn't. He walked away but watched you from afar. Could not believe your kindness, your empathy, the fact that you didn't ask a single question."

"Sometimes all you need is a smile."

"You told him that. You told him that being sad was no excuse for not being happy. Told him to smile, that it would get better."

"I don't really remember what I said."

"He remembered."

"What happened to him?"

"Everything. In a span of an afternoon he'd lost everything that mattered to him. His wife, his daughter, everything."

Sophie's eyes filled, she felt a tightening in her throat, looked around, her eyes landed on two graves next to Douglas'. His wife and his daughter. The year she'd met him. The year they'd died.

"See, he understood my pain. He took me under his wing. Me and Olivia. He was an amazing man."

"Is it weird to you that he gave me the cottage? That he didn't leave it to Olivia?"

Alex smiled. "No."

"No?"

"He always knew he was going to leave it for you."

"Why?"

"He knew."

"What did he know?"

"That you'd be an awesome neighbor, of course."

Sophie smiled. "Am I?"

"Are you what?"

"An awesome neighbor?"

"You're something of a neighbor," he said. She laughed.

A few moments passed in silence, then Sophie looked at Alex. "Do you miss him?"

His eyes clouded. "Every day."

Sophie moved closer to Alex, wrapped her arms around his shoulders. The sadness in his heart melted a little, morphed into warmth.

Like this, Alex thought, *exactly like this*.

Chapter Twelve

Alex

Alex had locked himself in, worked, stayed away from everybody. He'd gone to Liam's Pub after the cemetery. Alone. Peggy, well into her second beer, had been there. At the bar. She'd tried to kiss him. He walked away. Reminded her it was over. She started calling. Non-stop. He'd told her every which way he could that it was not going to happen. That he would never love her. Asked her to leave him alone. She'd finally listened, after one particular hard' conversation at the market. She'd followed him in, cornered him. He'd been blunt.

"Peg, enough. You knew this was the deal. I never lied."

"But Alex."

"No buts, Peggy. It's done. We will never happen."

"Alex, please."

"No! Stop following me, and don't call me again!"

He'd said it loud enough for everyone to hear. He'd felt bad, but she needed to understand. That had been three days ago. Peggy had stopped calling. She finally got it. Relieved, he looked out the window of his workshop. The sun had started to melt into the water. Orange, pink, yellow tinted the horizon. He stopped

45

sanding the new table, looked down. Out of the corner of his eye, he spotted his new neighbor. *Lovely*, he thought. She looked up at the sun, sipped a flute of pink bubbly that mimicked the color of the sky. Her feet tapped to the rhythm of something she was listening to. He could not hear the tune, ear buds, he assumed. Sophie got up from the chair, put her glass down, started dancing. He felt her joy. She took the steps down to her garden, twirled, sang the words to 'Dancing in the Moonlight', uninhibited. He could hear her voice a little out of tune. Thought of the phrase, *dance like no one is watching*. Except he was. Watching her. He smiled. He watched. Until the dancing stopped.

Moments later, he marched from his porch to hers, half bottle of red, glass in hand. He hadn't talked to her since seeing her at Douglas' grave. Realized he'd missed her. There she was, lost in the colors of the sunset.

"Hey," he said.

She looked his way, smiled.

"Hey neighbor. Can you believe all this beauty?" she said, looked back at the sun melting in the water.

"You got some moves," he said, took the seat next to hers.

"You saw?"

"I did."

She pressed her lips together, hid a smile that promised to escape.

"Everybody should dance in the almost moonlight at least once a week, I say."

"Is that so?"

"How long has it been?" she asked. "Since you danced?"

"In the moonlight?"

"Anywhere," Sophie looked at him.

"I don't really dance."

"Everybody dances."

"Hmmm," he said.

They watched in silence. After what seemed to be a long time to him, Sophie stirred.

"You want some ice cream?"

"Ice cream?"

"Good substitute for sex," she said.

Alex choked on his wine. God she was funny.

"I'm sorry, Alex, I just assumed, since you're sitting here with your neighbor, that you don't have a girlfriend at this particular time in your life. Ice cream does it for me. Can't you just tell? Just look at my hips, my tummy, and yes, yes, yes, my boobs. All made out of ice cream love."

Took him a few moments to stop coughing and laughing.

"What flavor?"

Sophie smiled. "Well, let's see... I can offer you Strawberry Cream, Chocolate Peanut Butter, Dulce de Leche, Carmel Cone and... yes, Coffee."

He looked at her, standing, not even aware of what she'd said. Adorable.

"So no to sex?"

"I wasn't offering, you oaf," she said.

"You sure? I may be able to assist you there, Sophie Alexander. With pleasure."

"Stop. You know what I mean."

"Do I?"

"Yes. You do."

"You sure now?"

"I'm going for Strawberry Cream today." She started to cross away.

"Bring two spoons."

Chapter Thirteen

Alex

Much later that night Alex walked into Liam's Pub. Restless, impatient, he needed something. Someone to relieve some of the pressure.

"Hey man," Liam said from behind the bar. "Where you been?"

"Busy building things."

"Breaking hearts," Liam said.

Alex looked at him.

"Yes, Peggy's been here. Every night. Waiting for you, dude. What's up with that? She has a body to die for and a face... You blind or something?" Liam said.

"Nah, just done there."

"Always done," Liam said.

"You know me."

"I do. So, what'll be?"

"Whiskey," Alex said.

Liam poured two fingers in a small glass. "How's Olivia?" Liam asked, careful.

"Good," Alex said.

"She have a boyfriend yet?" Looked past Alex, nodded to someone at the end of the bar.

"Nope."

Liam pulled the lever, filled a tall glass with dark Ale, placed it in front of one of the patrons crowding the bar. The Pub was hopping. A group of tourists in the corner table laughed.

"Good looking bunch," Liam said.

Alex nodded.

"Dibs on the blonde one by the window," Liam said.

"Way out of your league, man," Alex said.

"Want to bet?"

This is what they did. They'd been friends almost from the moment Alex landed in town. Didn't matter that Liam was twelve years younger. Liam worked at the Pub then, had not bought it yet. That came later, when Liam's grandfather sold it to him for way less than it was worth.

"You're on."

Chapter Fourteen

Alex

The sexy blonde had gone with Liam. He settled for the redhead. Still beautiful, smaller tits but feisty. He loved redheads. But Liam didn't need to know that. He needed a win. Alex spent the better part of the night at her hotel in a sexual marathon. The woman and her legs, her tongue, her ass. He was going to be tired, but the pressure was gone.

Still dark outside, she snored, soft. Alex untangled his body from hers, dressed, snuck out of the room. Easy. No entanglements. The redhead was from Seattle. She and the blonde were going back home today. Worked for him.

Alex stepped into the elevator, grabbed his phone, texted.

Alex: Owe you dinner, asshole.

An immediate ding.

Liam: Yeah you do!

Alex: Hope Blondie didn't disappoint. Red had moves that surprised me.

Liam: No complaints here.

Alex: So... steak?

Liam: And lobster. Thursday night. Basketball, then dinner.

Alex: A bet is a bet.
Liam: Yeah, and who won this bet?
The elevator door opened, Alex shook his head, smiled, put his phone in his pocket and stepped into the lobby.

Chapter Fifteen

Sophie

Friday morning Sophie sat by the window at the café. Lu had just left, off to Portland, business with her lawyer about one of her properties in Italy. Sophie lingered, enjoyed the slight soreness of a body happy from a yoga workout. Latte, half almond croissant left on her plate. Heaven. She closed her eyes for a moment, enjoyed the noise around her. The drip of the espresso machine, the hiss of the spout frothing milk, the ding of the register. Took in the scent of fresh brewed coffee, of sugar. The simple pleasures in life. No more rushing to work, mediating disputes between employees, hiring new faces eager to start their careers, overtime, always overtime. She didn't miss the rat race. Somehow, in the span of a month and a half, she'd settled into the life of a lady of leisure. She liked the sound of that, lady of leisure. Conjured all sorts of images, some innocent, some not.

"What's so funny?" Sophie heard the familiar voice of her next-door neighbor. Eyes flew open. "You look like the cat who just feasted on a pot of warm milk," Alex said.

"You would be right, sir," lifted her latte, took a sip. "Umm, not so hot anymore."

"I'll get you another one, okay?"

She nodded. "Thank you."

"But when I get back you have to tell me what made you smile."

"Maybe," she said, half-smile brightened her face.

"One splenda," Alex stated. She gave him a quizzical look. "I pay attention," he said, soft, stepped away.

He sure did. Pay attention, she thought. Not for one second was she looking at his ass walking away from her. Sexy in the tight jeans that allowed her to imagine. Nope, she wasn't looking, or wanting. Nope. *He's seven years younger than you, silly. Seven.* Okay, so seven years, almost eight Sophie reminded herself, was not such a big deal. Who was she kidding? It was a huge deal. Huge as in neighbor, gorgeous hunk who'd never look at her that way. What way? The way she longed someone looked at her since she was eleven. Since she'd watched 'Sabrina.' The one with Audrey Hepburn and Humphrey Bogart. She imagined herself Audrey Hepburn. Yes, Audrey lived in her soul, because in her body, impossible. The size of her boobs alone clear evidence of how not like Audrey she was.

"Still smiling that Mona Lisa smile, Sophe," Alex said, took the seat in front of her.

Sophe? She liked it coming out of his mouth.

"Am I?"

"Yes."

She looked at his face, he looked at her. Seconds watching, sizing up, saying nothing.

"So... tell me," he said.

"Audrey Hepburn."

He furrowed his brow, confused.

"How similar we are," twinkle in her eye.

"You and Audrey Hepburn? Yes, I can see it," twinkle matched hers.

"Yes, right? Same body, same face, same boobs."

He let out a laugh that had Rita, the barista, turn to look at them.

"Of course," he said, cough-laugh.

"Hey, a girl can dream and imagine herself any way she likes."

"What's wrong with the Sophie I see?"

"Hello, have you met me?"

"Not all of you, apparently. Haven't met your Audrey Hepburn boobs."

Her turn to laugh.

Suzy, Rita's daughter, brought over a coffee, a latte, a chocolate croissant.

"Thank you, Suzy," Alex smiled. Suzy beamed.

Sophie's eyes lit up when she saw the pastry.

"I'll share if you tell me what you were really thinking about," he said, serious.

"I was thinking about how much my life has changed in the last couple of months. No more work. Don't get me wrong. I loved working, but I kind of love being a slug as well."

"A slug?"

"Yep. Just... a lady of leisure, nothing to do, well I have plenty to do, but just what I love to do, you know?"

"I do know. In my former life I was a lawyer."

"You? Hmm. I guess if I really looked I could see it," squinted her eyes, scrunched her nose. "Yep, there it is, on the left eye, the glint of know-it-all power."

Alex laughed, she smiled.

"Never quite fit me, the life, you know," he said after a quiet moment. "I was good at it. Really good, but it didn't make me happy. It was expected of me, family business and all."

"Your dad?"

"And his father."

"Ah. So how did you end up making furniture?"

"My mom's father was a carpenter. Built beautiful furniture. I loved spending time with him on the weekends. He taught me," his eyes shone with nostalgic sadness.

"Why does it make you sad?"

"Cause he died when I was twelve. And it all stopped then. No more wood, no more..." he trailed off.

"No more dreams," Sophie finished his sentence.

"Exactly."

"Ah, but look at what you've done here."

"How do you know what I've done here?"

"I've heard, because you, Mr. Sexy Carpenter, have not invited me to see your workshop, or shown me your work. Who knows, I could be one of your future customers. Still furnishing a cottage, you know."

"You think I'm sexy?"

Such a man. Really? Only heard the one word in all she said.

"I don't but all the girls behind the counter do. They talk about you. Suzy has a huge crush on you."

"She's twelve!"

Suzy spent time at the café, drooled every time Alex walked through the door.

"So? Twelve year olds can be in love. Really in love."

"Speak from experience?'

"Of course. Intense kind of love, the one that leads a woman of twelve to sit in her room, in the dark, listen to

David Cassidy sing 'I think I love You' over and over again, imagine he sings just to her."

"David Cassidy, eh?"

"My third love." He looked at her. "I started early."

Alex grabbed a knife, cut the croissant in four, handed a small piece to Sophie.

"Thank you," she said, took a small bite, closed her eyes, "Mmmm."

"So you want to see my work?" Alex asked.

"I do. I may even want to buy some."

"Oh, I don't think you could afford my work."

"Really?"

"Really," his eyes twinkled with mirth.

"So..." she said.

"What?"

"How did you decide? To make the change, you know, from formal, serious attorney, tie and all, cause I can imagine you were, to a free-spirited man who works with his hands, wears t-shirts, lives by the sea, charms all the ladies?"

He smiled, then his eyes glazed a bit, he cleared his throat.

"I-did I say something that-"

"No, no, Sophe, you didn't. It's just that I haven't spoken about it, about the reason."

"No?"

"No."

"You don't have to tell me."

"It's okay. I want to," he took a minute or two to continue. Sophie leaned back, patient. "I guess when Mattie died so young, it forced me to reassess my life. Compelled me to think of what made me happy, when happiness was gone. I had Olivia to look after. I wanted to be able to be with her, all the time. I needed her just as much as she needed me and I realized life is short, sometimes shorter than we anticipate, and I had to make it count. My grandfather's words filled my ears. 'Alex, you see this piece of wood? Needs tending to, needs love, needs you to give it life.' I needed something to give life to, since my life was gone," shrugged his shoulders, half-smile, eyes a little misty.

Sophie's heart tightened. She leaned in, ran one finger down his cheek. "I'm so sorry, Alex. Really. I can't imagine."

Alex grabbed her finger, wrapped his hand around hers, squeezed. Cloud dissipated from his face.

"Yeah, well, Miss Audrey Hepburn, it was a long time ago. And I think this lemon has made a few lemonades since then."

She laughed. "Alex, that is the worst line ever. Ever!"

"As bad as 'Let me show you my furniture, little girl?'"

Chapter Sixteen

Alex

Thursday morning, father daughter hike. This was one of the things they did together, and they did many things together. It'd been just the two of them for a long time now. Now it was him alone at home. Olivia had moved out when she'd turned twenty-one.

"Time to spread my wings, Alex," she'd announced the day she got her job at 'Yoga For Life'.

"Do you have to?"

"You know I do, and besides, if I do maybe you'll get serious about one of your bimbos."

Never.

Now they hiked, bowled, watched movies, had dinner, lunch, anything and everything she wanted to do as long as she spent time with him, except go to the Pub. For some reason Olivia always made an excuse when he suggested they meet there. He didn't get it but okay, he respected her wishes.

Today he was puffing up the hill of one of their favorite trails in the Pacific Northwest. Trees, trees, more trees and Olivia urging him to keep up his pace. Damn twenty-four year old yoga master! Flexible and fast.

"Old man, you're running behind. Sexy night?"

"Olivia!"

"What, Alex? Haven't heard much about your new girl-toy. You're losing your touch."

"Yeah, well, you know I don't do that."

"Oh I know. Two weeks tops, if they're lucky."

"You're my daughter, we should not be talking about his."

"Puffing you mean? You can barely keep up today. What's up?"

What was up? He'd had a little trouble sleeping. Sophie's face kept popping up in his head. For no reason. Irked him a little.

"So... question."

"Yes dad, I'm dating, thank you very much."

"I don't want to know."

"What then? What do you want to know?"

"So... Sophie, you know, my neighbor -"

Olivia slowed down, laughed, looked at him.

"I know she's your neighbor. I know you two spend a lot of time together. Is she the reason you're not hooking up?"

"God, no! Sophie's just a friend, that's all. No. Never." Why had he even started?

"I know, Dad, I know. No way you'll ever be in a relationship again, blah, blah, blah. And God forbid with someone like her."

"Olivia, Sophie's great."

"Great? Sophie's fantastic. Lu and I adore her. She's truly a breath of fresh air. Kind of naive if you ask me, but adorable."

That she was. Adorable.

"Naive? I think she's smart."

"She is but so unaware of her surroundings sometimes."

"What do you mean?"

"Like she has no idea men find her attractive."

Men? Of course men found her attractive. He did. He was a man.

"She's lovely," he said.

"And sexy."

Sexy? Hell yes.

"Like we were at the club the other day and Edgar was flirting with her."

Edgar? Owner of the hardware store?

"He's too old for her," Alex said.

"Oh, is he?"

"Yes," Alex said.

"Well, she barely noticed him. Denied it when we told her."

Edgar. Nope. Not for Sophie.

"See, smart. Not right for her."

"Lu and I think she needs a boy-toy. But it was fun to see him try so hard and she simply let it all slip over her head, never took the bait. Then there was the time when we were at the sushi place..."

Something tightened in his belly. Olivia noticed his face. Took off up the hill.

"You want to know, you have to catch me."

Did he? Want to know?

Chapter Seventeen

Sophie

Another evening watching the sunset. Another evening Alex joined her. Tenth in a row. They had a rhythm. He'd show up with his bottle of wine, glass, pint of ice cream, two spoons. Sometimes they were quiet. Sophie always knew when Alex wanted to sit in silence, enjoy the view. With her. Sometimes they'd talk. Today Sophie wanted to talk. She could not understand why he was still alone. She got that he missed his Mattie, but he was a beautiful man with so much to offer.

"Still no girlfriend," Sophie said, took the ice cream.

"Not even a question. A statement."

"So that's a no?"

He nodded.

"So, eleven years, five months, sixteen days," Sophie said.

Alex froze, turned to look at Sophie.

"I pay attention," she smiled, reached for his hand. Felt his pain in her heart. "Alex, I don't mean to overstep, I know we barely know each other, but I want to talk to you about something. You can tell me to mind my own business, but-"

"Mattie's everything to me."

"I know. But it's been a long time. Olivia told me you've been alone. No girlfriend. No relationships."

"I've had company."

"But nothing real."

"No."

"Why?"

Sophie recognized the struggle on his face, the tension in his shoulders.

"Alex, it's okay, we don't have to talk today. Just, you know, I've come to know you a little bit and I think you're great. I like you, very much, feel we are forging a friendship, and I can't help but wonder. You've got so much to give. There's a woman out there who could make you happy, who -"

"No, Sophie, no," Alex interrupted, removed his hand from under hers. "There's no one out there. Mattie's it for me. I don't want anybody else. I want Mattie. I want her."

"But she's gone."

"Don't you think I know that? Every day I know that." Alex downed his glass of wine, got up, started to walk away.

"I'm sorry," Sophie said, soft.

"Sorry?" He stopped.

"For asking. For poking in your wound. I'm sorry, Alex. This is your story. Your life. I had no right to ask."

"Sophie," his back to her.

"It's okay. Go. Just know that if you ever want to talk, I've got ice cream."

Alex stood there, did not move a muscle.

"Go. You won't hurt my feelings. Go."

He did. Walked away, slow. Sophie felt a hand press on her heart, felt his pain. She shook her head, vowed never to ask again.   She liked spending time with him. She'd gotten used to their evenings, their talks, their laughs. Not today. There'd been no laughter today. On her. She'd wanted to know.   She'd asked but this part of him was closed to her. Maybe to everybody. No discussion.

Sophie grabbed her glass, walked into her cottage.

Chapter Eighteen

Alex

Alex plopped himself at the bar, in front of Liam. The Pub was busy. Liam placed a double whiskey in front of Alex, said nothing.

"Thanks," Alex said, winced as the liquid traveled down his throat, burned a little.

Liam pulled a couple of beers, delivered them to patrons on the other side of the bar, motioned for the other bartender to cover for him, grabbed the bottle, a glass for himself, took the stool next to Alex.

"Alex?" Liam said.

Alex looked at his friend, brow furrowed.

"What's up, man?" Liam asked.

Alex cleared his throat, shook his head.

"Is it Peggy? She up your ass again?"

"No."

"What is it then? Don't think I've ever seen you so shaken up."

"Sophie," Alex whispered.

"Sophie? Your next door neighbor?"

"I want to be mad at her, really mad, but I can't."

"Why do you want to be mad at her?"

"She... she asks all these questions, looks at me with these big beautiful caring eyes and..."

"About Mattie?"

Alex closed his eyes, nodded, swallowed.

"Alex, why would Sophie be asking you questions about Mattie?"

"We've been spending time together."

"You and Sophie? Is that why you dumped Peggy?"

Alex opened his eyes. "No!"

"No?"

"She and I are friends."

"Friends?"

"Just friends. Nothing more."

"Ah," Liam said. "And?"

"We've been spending a lot of time together. I mean, she's sweet. I like her energy. She makes me laugh, when she's not asking questions. We watch the sunset together, drink, eat ice cream."

"That's why we haven't played basketball? Because you've been eating ice cream with your neighbor?"

"No, yes."

Liam said nothing, stared.

"It's not how you think, man. Really. We're just friends. I-she-I like spending time with her."

"You haven't slept with her?"

"No! No, it's not like that. No. Friends. Only friends."

"If you say so," Liam said.

Chapter Nineteen

Sophie

The following morning Sophie met Lu at yoga. She'd had a bad night. Felt awful for intruding in Alex's life. Alex had not come back. She'd not seen him this morning. He always jogged past her when she took her morning walk. Always touched her back, startled her, laughed, then ran by. Not today.

"So I put my foot in my mouth yesterday," Sophie said to Lu.

"With your sexy neighbor?"

"How did you know?"

"Oh, darling, you talk about him all the time. You two are connected."

"What? No. We're just friends."

"Mmm-hmm."

"Really, Lu, for God's sake he's seven years younger than me."

"So you've thought about this."

"Back to topic, please."

"Okay, what did you say?"

"I told him it'd been a long time since his wife died, asked why he didn't have a girlfriend."

"What did he say?"

"That Mattie was the only one for him, then he walked away."

Olivia walked into class, hugged Sophie.

"Olivia, I think I upset your dad last night. You should check on him. Please," Sophie said.

"I spoke to him this morning. He's okay," Olivia said, walked to the front of the room to start class.

When class was over, Olivia said to Sophie and Lu. "Tea time, I think."

Sophie breathed easier, she wanted to talk to Olivia about Alex. She could not shake the feeling that she had put a block between them and she'd gotten used to their comfortable, easy friendship. And his smile.

Chapter Twenty

Alex

He stopped across the street from the Café. Olivia, Lu and Sophie sat at their favorite table. Sophie. Damn! He wasn't ready to face Sophie today. She'd nicked at his wound, forced him to think about his life. Nobody talked to him that way. Asking questions without wanting to take from him. Just wanting to understand. Wanting him to understand. He knew that, yet, he wasn't ready.

That's why Olivia called, asked him to meet her for coffee. Wanted him to make peace with Sophie. He did, too. Make peace. Forget about the past. Focus on the present.

Olivia spotted him, waved him over. He watched as Sophie caught sight of him, offered a half-smile. Shook his head, ran across the street, entered the café. Olivia stood.

"Daddy," she kissed his cheek.

"Bad girl," he whispered in her ear.

Olivia laughed. Lu hugged him a little too tight.

"Hey," Sophie said, seated.

"Hey," he said, looked at her.

"Sorry," Sophie mouthed.

Alex smiled, nodded, the knot in his heart loosening a little.

"What do you want, Alex?" Olivia asked.

"I'll get it."

"Nope, let me. Coffee, chocolate croissant?"

"Sounds good."

"Be back," Olivia said, looked at Lu.

"Bathroom," Lu said, the two walked away.

Alex stood there for a moment, said nothing. Sophie shrugged. "I promise not to poke," she said. "I promise not to be such a baby," he said. "Truce," she extended her hand. "Truce," he took hers in his.

"I thought I was going to have to eat ice cream all by myself now," she said.

She knew exactly what to say to lighten any moment, to help him forget. To make him want... ice cream.

"Hey, Alex," Olivia said, taking her seat. "Sit."

Lu returned a second later. Took the chair next to Sophie, left Alex to take the seat across the table. He'd wanted to sit next to Sophie, to feel her energy mingle with his. *Better this way*, he thought.

Food arrived. Alex cut a piece of his croissant, offered it to Sophie. A peace offering, a bridge. She yelped, delighted, accepted the pastry.

"Our Sophie does love her sweets," Lu said.

"How about a hike? To offset all this sugar," Olivia said.

"A hike? How hard of a hike? Knowing you and Lu, I'll be out of breath in two minutes."

"I know an easy one. Beautiful path," Alex said.

Alex caught the look Lu gave Olivia. An 'I told you so' look.

"What? I like to hike," he said.

Chapter Twenty-one

Sophie

*S*tunning, Sophie thought. The views, the path, the company. Alex and Olivia raced up the trail, competitive, pushed each other, playing like the father and daughter they were. Lu stayed with Sophie. They'd been on the trail for about an hour.

"Sorry, Lu, you can step it up if you like. I'm not there yet."

"Nonsense. Good to just take in the air, smell the flowers, stroll. Let those two knock each other out."

"Hmmm," Sophie said.

"Great ass," Lu said, staring at Alex's backside.

"Yep. All in all, perfect package."

"Perfect package for you?"

"No Lu."

"Wouldn't you love to be caught between those legs? Naked?"

Alex and Olivia headed back towards them.

"Stop!" Sophie blushed. She kind of would.

"No?"

"No."

"No what?" Alex said.

"Lu," Sophie warned.

"Nothing," Lu said, winked at Sophie.

Alex slowed his pace to match Sophie's. Olivia kept hers up. Lu took after her, left Sophie to turn, walk back with Alex.

"You don't have to slow down for me, Alex. Go," Sophie said.

"Second day you've told me to go."

He matched her.

"Oh."

They walked in silence for a bit.

"So what's a 'no' Sophie?"

God, what would she say? She couldn't tell him what they'd been talking about. The images that leaped in her head, their bodies, naked, sweaty. Nope.

"It was nothing," she said.

"Then tell me."

"Race you," Sophie said, sped up her pace down the trail. She heard him laugh, catch up to her.

"Coward," he whispered, took her hand, slowed his run to match her pace.

Chapter Twenty-two

Sophie

Sophie, in bed, dialed Annie's number. They hadn't talked in a few days. She missed her friend, although she had new friends now. Good friends.

"Sophe," Annie answered.

"Too late?"

"Nope. Was about to call you myself. Guess what? John got the promotion."

Sophie smiled, happy. "Wow, happy for him, but does that mean you're moving?"

"For a couple of years, yes."

John worked for an international firm. Their main headquarters in Florida.

"Miami, Annie, really?"

"Getting my spa wardrobe ready," Annie said.

"But Miami?"

"Shut up!"

A silent moment. "I'm gonna miss you," Sophie whispered.

"You can come visit. I'll find you an old, rich, New York geezer and plan your wedding."

"That would be awesome!"

"Right?" Annie said.

"When?"

"In two weeks. We've known for a while."

"Why didn't you tell me?"

"Sophe, just wanted to see how you got along. But now I know I have nothing to worry about."

"I'm coming to see you tomorrow."

"Stay the night?"

"Of course."

Chapter Twenty-three

Alex

Alex paced looking out the window. No Sophie yet. She'd missed sunset the last two days. He'd called. She'd texted back. She'd gone to Portland to see Annie. He knew all about Annie, Sophie's best friend. Annie was moving, Sophie said.

Alex wandered into his kitchen, opened the freezer, grabbed a pint of Mint Chip, only one spoon. When would she be back? How come he missed her?

The sound of a car, he went to the window. Her car. She pulled into the driveway.

"Hey, Sophe," he said, rushing to open her door.

"Alex, hi, what are you doing here?"

"I missed you," he said, offered a spoonful of ice cream.

"Mmmm," she said, "delicious."

"How did it go?"

"A little sad. Going to miss driving to Portland to see her, but this is good for her and John. Just the two of them. Romantic, really."

"Want to talk?"

"How about I go in, change, meet you and we don't talk."

"Is this a proposition?"

Sophie laughed, blushed.

"No!"

"Why not?"

"This is an invitation to bubbly, or in your case, red and ice cream."

"Sunset?"

"And a little dancing in the moonlight," she said.

Later, she had pulled him up the chair, played the song, forced him to dance with her. Not a romantic dance. A silly, vibrant, happy dance. She'd twirled him, he'd stepped on her foot. She'd laughed. *A friendship dance*, he'd thought.

Chapter Twenty-four

Sophie

"Aw, Lu, I'm not sure," Sophie said, doing an about face, glided away from Lu.

"Hey, hey! Get back here!"

"I'm not sure, Lu. I'm really not."

"*Fifona! Sei una gran fifona.*"

"You know I don't speak Italian."

Lu clucked like a chicken, flapped her arms.

"Really? What are you, five?" Sophie said.

"Multiply by ten, *cara*. Don't you forget it."

"Lu."

"Sophie."

"Maybe tomorrow, okay?"

"Nope. It's today. Today is your day. Didn't you tell me you've always wanted a tattoo? Didn't you say good-bye to the old Sophie, didn't we toast to being fearless? For fuck's sake, Sophie, we polished a whole bottle of Prosecco. You're having a big birthday soon."

"Not that soon. Still have six more months in my fifties, so I have time before I do something to my body I can't take back."

"*Fifona!*"

"Lu!"

"Didn't a certain *ragazza* tell me she wanted to do something out of character? Didn't she say she wanted to be fearless? Daring? Didn't she tell me she wanted ink before she turned sixty? Well, it's now or never, Sophie. This is what separates the boys from the men."

"I'm a woman, Lu, my boobs should give you a clue."

"Yes, and they are magnificent, darling, so... let's put some ink on them. Benjamin's going to love decorating you."

Benjamin's work spoke for itself. Olivia's butterfly, exquisitely drawn, colored in blues, gold, inspired Sophie. Lu's martini glass, three olives, liquid dripping droplets down the course of Lu's scar, red lips, brought warmth and a smile to Sophie's face every time she saw it. So Lu. Humorous, sophisticated, eccentric, emotional. Three olives depicted three husbands gone. Each took a piece of her heart. The drops of liquid down the scar on her back, kissing the pain of the accident, the loss of Davide, Lu's first husband, the love of her life. Sophie knew the story. They'd been crazy in love. Reckless. That recklessness took his life, marked her with a physical and emotional scar.

Destroyed Lu until she met Giulio, her second husband. A beautiful, gentle soul who healed her pain with his love. After him came Tony, her American husband, the reason she ended up in Oregon. Then a string of young and older lovers. Lu loved love. She had stories. The gorgeous Benjamin, his enormous... package one of them.

"Dragonfly? Ladybug? Chicken? What'll it be?"

"I – I don't know," Sophie said, overwhelmed, terrified.

"I say dragonfly, my *fifona*, the symbol of change. Time to change, *libellula*. The magnificent boob needs a little ink."

"Not the boob, no. The first one on the small of my back," Sophie said.

"Ah, so more than one then?"

"Let's start with one, okay?"

"Okay, let's," Lu pulled Sophie into the shop. Small. Tidy. Beautiful, mysterious artwork on the walls. Sophie heard the buzz of the machine in use in the back room.

"I think he's busy," Sophie's voice trembled a little.

The buzzing stopped. A few seconds later, the most amazing looking man walked out to the reception area of Benjamin's Tattoo. Tall, muscular, skin the color of gold, sparkling green-gray eyes, intricate, artistic designs covered his arms. Still room for more. Young.

Sophie's throat closed, she turned to Lu, whispered, "You didn't tell me he was gorgeous."

"I did, *cara*, you just weren't listening."

"I-I can't."

"You can," Lu said, turned to Benjamin who'd been watching their exchange, "Benjamin, darling." Kissed him square on the lips.

"*Principessa*, a delight to see you again so soon," Benjamin said, British accent. Sophie loved an accent, a British one made her weak in the knees, but one coming out of a Celtic God, well, that kind of rendered her speechless.

"Remember I told you about my Sophie? That she needed an original from you?"

"I remember. So you've brought the magnificent Sophie to me?" He turned to Sophie, "Hello beautiful. What are we doing today?"

Sophie cleared her throat, "Ahem, well, I – Lu – I, have been thinking of a – ah –"

"Your first," Benjamin said.

"A tattoo virgin," Lu said. Sophie closed her eyes.

"Yes, and I'm a little –"

"Nervous. I get it," Benjamin said. "I promise I'll be gentle. What would you like?" He said, soothing.

"A dragonfly."

"And where is this dragonfly going to live?"

"The small of my back."

"Perfect spot," he smiled. "Give me five minutes to finish with my client. Then I'll design something relevant for you."

He strode into his back room. Sophie's feet started mopping the floor, slow at first, then gaining speed, moving towards the entrance. Lu leaped to the frame of the front door, creating a barrier between the shop and Sophie's freedom.

"Lu."

"Sophie."

"Please..."

"Courage, darling."

"But you'll stay with me, right? You'll go back with me?"

"Of course I will."

More pacing.

"That fitbit's going to hit its mark and it's not even noon," Lu said.

"Shut up! I'm nervous."

"I can see that."

"You will stay with me, Lu. You will."

"I said I would."

More pacing. The buzzing stopped in the back. A beautiful woman walked out, beaming.

"Ben is awesome," she said.

"Oh, yes, he is," Lu said.

Sophie's heart raced with the adrenalin of fear. She inched towards the door, hoped Lu would not catch her.

"*Fifona*! I see you."

Sophie, right foot out the door, froze, closed her eyes, took a breath, walked back in. "I can do this. I can," she whispered. "I. Can. Do. This."

"Yes you can," Benjamin whispered in her ear. Sophie jumped.

"Ah-oh-hmm yes," Sophie said.

"C'mon, gorgeous, let's paint some beauty on this sexy bod."

"Lu..." Sophie said.

"Yes, Sophie, coming."

Benjamin stopped, looked at Lu. "Lu," he said, "This is something the gorgeous Sophie needs to do alone. Come back in an hour." He grabbed Sophie's hand, pulled her to the back room. Sophie's eyes turned to Lu's. She mouthed, *please*. Lu lifted her shoulders, winked, turned, walked out of the shop.

Chapter Twenty-five

Sophie

The design, exquisite. Dragonflight, he called it. "For the beginning of your flight of change, lovely," Benjamin said. Diaphanous wings with a hint of pink, bejeweled body in sparkling turquoise, aquamarine eyes. Mesmerized by the design, Sophie sighed, it tugged at her heart, her spirit. Even more beautiful than she had imagined. Fitting for the change she'd been looking for. This was it.

Benjamin prepared the colors, the machine, the light to begin his masterpiece. Sophie examined his body, his face, could not help but feel small next to this gorgeous man. *This is what God creates when She's in a good mood,* she thought.

"Okay, lovely, it's time. Lean on the bed here, pull down your pants."

Sophie's heart stopped for a second. She hadn't thought it through. Pull her pants down? He'd see her humongous bottom. Not ready for that, never would be. Nope. Nobody'd seen that bottom in a long time. She cleared her throat. "Not-not all the way, right?" She said. Benjamin smiled, a hint of fun in his eye.

"As low as you're comfortable, gorgeous."

Sophie turned away from Benjamin, pulled the back of her leggings down a bit, just to over the top of her crack, opened her legs for balance, leaned forward until her forearms rested on the tattoo bed, anchoring her.

"Perfect spot for the Dragonflight, Sophie. Perfect. So soft. You are so very soft," Benjamin said, cleaned the spot with an alcohol-drenched cotton ball. Traced her skin with his fingertips, sensual.

Sophie's mind went straight to her weight. He meant she was 'pillowy', chubby.

"Ready?"

"Y-yes."

"Okay then."

Sophie felt a piece of paper on her back, Ben traced the image onto her skin. She closed her eyes. Oh God, her butt was right in front of his face. Humiliating. Could she have picked a different place on her body? Her shoulder? No, no, she had to choose her lower back. Why?

"Why not?" Benjamin said. What the hell? Was he a mind reader or had she said it out loud? She turned her head, looked at him. Found his eyes, felt his finger touching her skin, soft. Her right leg started to tremble. She'd always heard of people trembling uncontrolled, she'd thought it was bullshit. It could be controlled. She ordered her leg to stop, but her leg had developed a mind of its own. Refused. The buzz of the machine. Benjamin repositioned the light on her ass, started to work. She felt the needle begin, gentle. Huh. No pain. Getting your bikini waxed, pain. Electrolysis, pain. Benjamin's needle, the opposite of pain. A caress. An image. Alex's teeth grazing her skin, dropping little kisses, making designs with his lips. Her eyes flew open. Alex! Where did he come from? She was with sexy Benjamin. Gorgeous Benjamin was staring at her ass. Not Alex.

Oh no. Her left leg joined in the dance. Shaking. Shit. Shit. Shit. She ordered both legs to stop. Behind her Benjamin giggled. The man giggles. How adorable, how sexy could he be?

"Relax, lovely. Not going to hurt you."

"Sorry. I don't know what's happening. My legs seem to have a life of their own."

"It's okay," he said, never took his eyes off his work.

Sophie tried really hard to relax. Truly. What the hell was wrong with her? She could control this. Her body needed to respond to her command, it could not go rogue on her. Nope.

Shaking got worse. The Buzzing continued, Benjamin's hands steady in their task. She turned back.

Looked at him. "Sorry," she said, "Don't know how to make them stop."

Buzzing stopped. Eyes met hers, mischievous smile on his lips, hand patted his thigh, inviting Sophie to sit. Sophie gulped, turned forward, begged the trembling to stop. No way in hell she was going to sit on his lap. If she did, he'd know how much she weighed.

Chapter Twenty-six

Sophie

Lu and Olivia screamed in laughter when Sophie told them about Benjamin patting his thigh. They were at a restaurant by the sea celebrating Sophie's Dragonflight. Sophie downed her Cosmopolitan, ordered a second one.

"Liquid courage," Olivia said.

"You're an idiot!" Lu said.

"Who's an idiot?" Alex said, pulling the empty chair next to Sophie.

"What are you doing here?" Sophie asked, her mind recalling the fantasy of his teeth grazing her skin, heat on her cheeks.

"Olivia said you ladies were celebrating you not being a *fifona*. I wanted to celebrate, too. What did you do, Sophie? And what the hell is a *fifona*?"

"Sophie got a tattoo," Lu said, took a sip of her martini, ate one of the three olives in the glass.

Chapter Twenty-seven

Alex

"A tattoo? Of a chicken?" Alex said, took a sip of wine.

"No, not a chicken. You think I'd get a tattoo of a chicken?"

"Sophie, I don't think you're a chicken, but what do I know? Just a guy who doesn't understand women."

"She was very brave, but also a chicken. *Fifona*." Lu clucked like a chicken.

"Confused," Alex said.

"Benjamin put the moves on Sophie," Olivia said.

Alex tensed. Benjamin made a pass at Sophie? His Sophie? Something in his belly stirred.

"He did not!" Sophie said.

"Tell her, Alex. There she was, pants down, ass in his face-" Olivia said.

"My ass was not in his face!"

"Were you not leaning on the bed, legs spread, pants down?" Lu asked.

What the hell?

"Well, maybe but my pants were up. All he could see was the small of my back."

"You sure?" Lu said.

"Nothing more. This ass is private."

Her ass. A certain part of Alex's anatomy stirred at the thought of Sophie's soft-round form.

"Yeah, well, he invited you to sit on his lap," Lu said.

Alex's stomach flipped.

"You sat on his lap?"

"No!"

"Guess why, Alex. Guess," Olivia laughed.

He lifted his shoulders.

"*Fifona*," Lu said.

"Because she didn't want him to know how much she weighed. Tell her, Alex, tell her gorgeous Benjamin made a pass, she could have had the most delicious hot sex with that hunk of a man. Tell her she's an idiot," Olivia said.

Chapter Twenty-eight

Alex

Alex waited all afternoon to join Sophie on the back porch. He'd been so relieved she hadn't had sex with Benjamin. The thought of the young man running his hands on her softness, her curves, her breasts, riled him. Unsettled him.

He looked out the window, wanted to see her. He grabbed the wine, his glass, headed out the back to her place.

He found her wrapped in a cozy blanket. His heart fluttered. Lovely. Seemed to him the more he knew her the more he liked her. Liked. That was all. A friendship like. Nothing more.

"Hey stranger," she said.

"Might I interest you on a lap to sit? Mine is very comfortable," he took the seat beside hers, patted his thigh.

"Stop," she blushed.

Adorable.

"So you really turned down young Benjamin's offer for sex?"

"That's not what it was. He was just teasing."

"Because you thought he'd know how much you weighed," Alex chuckled, releasing the tension logged in his heart. "Sophie, the boy wanted you."

"You said it. Boy. And no. He did not want me. He was teasing me."

"You said that already."

"So I did."

"He was testing you to see if you actually would take him up on his offer."

"Pfft!"

"Sophie, Sophie, what do you see when you look at yourself in the mirror? You're beautiful. Soft, round in all the right places. Any man would be stupid not to see that. Not to want you."

"All this deliciousness, you mean? Yes, he wanted me to crush him with all of my 'deliciousness'."

"Stop."

Alex leaned back, took in the view. They were quiet for a moment. Shades of orange tinted the sky. You could almost hear the sun sizzle in the water.

"Wow, gorgeous," Sophie said.

"Yes," Alex said, eyes on her. When had he started to think of Sophie as more than a neighbor? When had he wanted to spend time with her? A lot of time. All of his time. He thought about her every single night. *Stop*, he thought. *Friends. Only friends. Just stop.* He shivered.

"Cold?" Sophie asked.

"A little," he said.

"Blanket on the couch, inside."

Alex nodded, rose, walked into her cottage.

"So *fifona*, when do I get to see the famous chicken?" Alex said moments later, blanket around his shoulders.

Sophie laughed. "You don't get to see the chicken."

"Why?" Plopped on his chair. His chair. When did the chair become his?

"Because it's not a chicken."

"Okay, so when do I get to see the ink on your ass?"

Sophie giggled. "It's not on my ass. It's my lower back. And you don't."

"Why?"

"Because you're not my young lover. Only my lover gets to see the Dragonflight."

"You mean dragonfly."

"Benjamin named it Dragonflight. For change. For beauty. For..."

Alex did not like to hear Benjamin's name on Sophie's lips.

"For sexy," he said. *For mine*, he thought.

"Hmmm."

"So when do I get to see this famous piece of ink art?" Alex asked.

"Uhmm, never," Sophie said.

Chapter Twenty-nine

Sophie

Dawn. Another favorite for Sophie. Today she decided to greet the day on her porch. She'd had a little trouble sleeping. Too much in her head. Too much Alex. Took a sip of her coffee, wrapped herself tighter in the blanket. Closed her eyes for a second.

"Morning, neighbor," Alex whispered, in case Sophie was asleep.

"Hey," she said, heart fluttered. "You're up early."

"So are you."

"I'm always up at this time of the day, just today figured I'd drink my coffee outside instead of in bed. It's cold, though."

"You need a fireplace out here."

"That's a brilliant idea!"

"I'd ask your favorite handyman if he'd be willing to build you one."

"Does he charge a lot for his work?"

"Depends."

"Hmm. Afraid to ask what it depends on."

"I think he'd do it for a glimpse of a certain tattoo."

"Then I guess it's a no."

"Think about it. Odds are in your favor."

He sat next to her.

"So quiet," she said.

"Yes."

Sophie struggled. She wanted to ask Alex about Mattie. About his vow to not love again. He'd been so mad last time she'd brought it up, but something told her it was time to start the conversation again.

"Spit it out, Sophie."

"What?"

"I can tell you want to ask me something." Wow! *He can read my energy*, she thought. *He knows me, maybe like no one else does.*

"But... you have to promise not to walk away. Promise not to be mad. Promise you'll let me ask, and you'll tell me only what you want me to know."

"Mattie," he stated.

"Yes, Alex, I'm sorry. It's been eating at me. I don't understand. It's been eleven years, seven months, two days."

"But who's counting," he said, soft.

"I don't want you to be sad. I want you to be happy. Truly happy. God, you are gorgeous. Smart. Funny. Kind. You need someone in your life. You need love."

"I have Olivia. I have you." Her heart thumped.

"You know what I mean."

"Sophie, when Mattie died, my world crumbled. I had a young daughter to take care of, needed to stay afloat. But the light went out. I loved her so much. So so much. No one could ever fill her spot. She died too young. Not fair."

Sophie reached over, touched his arm.

"I know. Okay, don't be mad, please, but Mattie's gone. You're still here. You deserve a second chance. Not just a hook-up here and there, but someone to have a life with. I feel it. You need it. Olivia's an adult now. You need someone."

"Do I?"

"Just think about it."

"Okay," he said.

He got up.

"You mad?"

"No," he said, dropped a kiss on Sophie's head. "Going for a run."

"Okay," she said.

Alex took a few steps, turned, smiled. "You think I'm gorgeous."

Chapter Thirty

Alex

"Have you ever been married?" Alex asked the following week. Nightfall, seated next to each other. He'd been itching to know more about her. Really get to know her. She knew everything he'd been willing to share about himself. He hoped Sophie would tell him all about herself. After all, she thought he was gorgeous. Smile reached his heart. Gorgeous. Hmmm. He kind of liked that.

"Once," Sophie whispered.

"When?"

"Long time ago."

"What happened?"

Sophie took a minute.

"You don't have to," Alex said, hoped she would.

"No, it's fine. I was young. He was young. We were not meant to be. Lasted five very long, unhappy years. Should have ended it after one. Only time in my life

I've been lonely. He wasn't bad. We were just not right, you know. Didn't fit."

"I get that."

"Do you?"

"I do."

"Really? Because you and Mattie. Perfect. The love of your life. I've never had that. Not sure I believe it's possible."

"You don't?"

Sophie shrugged. "But I have ice cream, my true, faithful, flawless boyfriend."

Alex smiled.

"And besides, love is always better in my head," she said, soft.

"Explain."

"Well, see, people are who they are, flawed, vulnerable, hurtful. But in my head, in my heart, I imagine the ideal one for me. A man who does not exist anywhere but in my imagination. He can be anyone I want him to be. He can be... Daniel Craig."

Alex raised an eyebrow. "Daniel Craig?"

"Gorgeous specimen of a man who loves me but doesn't know it yet," she stated.

Alex frowned. He looked nothing like Daniel Craig.

"In my head this man is perfect. Except he's not real," Sophie continued.

"So you've never been in love?"

"Sure I have. Lots of times."

"Hmmm." She'd been in love lots of times. Not sure how that settled in him. He wanted more. "Tell me, Sophe. I want to know."

She shrugged.

"I want to know what makes you happy," he said, soft, alert, intense.

"Happy, hmm, well, happy and love don't go together for me. It's never been... oh, I don't know how to say it. Maybe I've been waiting all my life for someone. Someone who is familiar. Someone who knows me, really knows me, sees the real me. Inside and out. Someone who wakes the butterflies in my stomach. Someone... oh, Alex, it's hard to put into words. No one has ever asked me before. I guess I need to work it out, to say it right."

"You just did," he said. "So... loved many times, but never been really in love."

"Yes," she said.

"And love and happy don't go together for you."

"Yes."

"And?" He asked.

"Okay, gonna tell you something but you're going to think I'm crazy, or from California."

"Intrigued. Go on."

"I think if anyone can understand this it's you, because of how you feel about Mattie still, after so many years. How she is the one and only one for you."

Alex's heart warmed. How this woman he had met only a few months before got him. Recognized his heart. No judgment. He liked her. A lot. Thought about her. A lot. Wanted to touch her. A lot.

"Tell me," reached for her hand. Found it.

"Well, I kinda, sort of, believe in past lives. Maybe. I believe and I don't believe, if you know what I mean."

"Say it, California."

"So I feel here," Sophie let go of his hand, placed hers over her heart. "That there is someone out there who I know from before. That is close, but not here. Don't know if he'll ever get here, but he is out there and we have something unfinished. Something that needs to begin again, and again, and again. I feel I've been walking through lives and just have not found him. He hasn't looked for me. My eyes, my heart, open, waiting. I just can't see him."

"And you haven't met him yet?"

"I don't think so," she took a beat. "Maybe. Maybe I met him and didn't recognize him."

"What do you mean?"

"Okay, when I was really young, twenty-one maybe, I was in love, or so I thought, with a guy. Bit of a womanizer, sexy as hell, dangerous. He was my first, you know."

"The first guy you slept with?"

"Yep."

"Twenty-one?"

"A little slow here," she said.

"No. Just surprised. Was it him?"

"No," she laughed. "Not him. But I was in love. Working at my first real job right after college. Assistant to the head of personnel. Morning break, wanted coffee, hadn't had much sleep the night before."

"Sophie," he winked.

"Yeah, yeah, relax. Yes. So, I walked out of the building, thinking about him, yes, Alex, about our night together, my first. A young man came running after me, grabbed my arm, turned me around and said, 'Who are you?' He startled me out of my daydream. I looked at him, looked away and scurried. He scared me. I think it may have been him. He didn't pursue me, though, but I never forgot that moment, that feeling. Always wondered if it was him."

"Him?"

"You know, the one. But I let him go. And he didn't follow me."

Alex looked at her, wanted to take her in his arms.

"So," she continued, "A couple of months before I moved here, I had my chart done."

"Chart?"

"Astrological chart. A gift from Annie for my fifty-ninth. This amazing woman, funny, insightful, told me about my life. She said I would be coming into some money, that my life would do an about face. She said I would finally live the life I was meant for. She said, and I quote, 'He will find you.' I was confused, asked what she meant. She told me about a past life, centuries ago, when we had been together but torn apart before we could form a life with each other. That we'd been looking for each other all these lifetimes. We have unfinished business, but this time he was my gift. All up to him, she said, up to him to find me, to want me. Up to me to be open. Unfinished love, she said, and somewhere inside me it made sense, you know."

Alex laughed, nervous.

"Okay, young man, you asked, I told you. You think all of this is bullshit, right?"

"I don't know, Sophie. One thing I do know, Mattie and I were meant for each other. We were so young. First day of High School. She was beautiful. She knew me. Pursued me. Got me. She was it for me. So maybe there's something to this past life stuff. Maybe."

"Your eyes soften when you talk about her."

"I love her."

"You miss her."

"Every day."

Sophie placed her hand over Alex's, squeezed. Alex turned his palm over, linked his fingers with hers. Her touch stirred something in him, something he pushed away, ignored, refused to see. Something he didn't know he wanted.

They watched the sun disappear into the water in silence.

"I do have one regret," Sophie said a few minutes later.

Alex turned, looked at her.

"Not sitting on Benjamin's lap," eyes twinkled.

"Maybe you should have. I hear impressive things about Big Ben."

Sophie threw her head back, laughed. Got up.

"Where are you going?"

"Boyfriend calling. Today I think it's chocolate peanut butter. You in?"

"Bring it on."

Chapter Thirty-one

Sophie

What on earth made her open up to Alex the way she did?

Sophie, coffee cup in hand, sat at the armchair near the window, looked out. Still dark. She had not turned on the light. Didn't want Alex to know she was awake.

What made her tell him? He had. Alex with his warm eyes, closed heart, open only for friendship. Friendship. That's all it would ever be. She knew. She'd always known. Love, always close, never there. Never for her. But Alex, Alex made her heart flutter. Last night she'd dreamt about him. His mouth on her mouth. His hands on her skin. She smelled his fresh, citrus scent mixed with man. Moaned under his body. Sexy. Hot. Dissolved before satisfaction. Dang! She'd have to shut the feelings down, the thoughts, the dreams. Off. Fast. Too many things against this. Alex, too young for her. Seven long years. A lifetime in dog years and she was insecure enough about her body to let the beautiful Alex anywhere near it. Besides, and most important, he didn't want her. He did not want anything real with a woman. Flings, yes. She was not sure she could survive a fling with him. Her heart definitely not. She liked him too much. Wait. She liked him? Sophie closed her eyes. Yes, she liked him. More than liked him, but she was an expert at keeping men she had feelings for at bay. Took a deep breath, visualized another layer of protection around her heart. The crust that had protected her all these years got thicker. It would crack only for the one, but it was too late for the one. She was going to be sixty for fuck's sake. Sixty! No place for love anymore, but why did she want it still? Because she wanted him, there was no denying it. They'd been spending too much time together. Their outings, their evenings sharing ice cream, words and sometimes silence. She needed distance. A couple of nights away from him to set her head straight, her heart. *Run away* whispered the coward in her head. *It's easier. Coward, run away from love.* Love? Who'd said anything about love? Sex, she meant sex, attraction. Not love. Yes, that was it. She wanted sex. Sex with Alex, his body on hers. Stop! Nope. No!

Hours later, Sophie walked into yoga. Lu was there already. She'd skipped her walk and spent the morning with frozen boyfriend of the day, the sweet Dulce de Leche.

"Hey Lu," Sophie said.

"Darling, you look like hell!"

"Good morning to you, Sunshine," Sophie laughed.

"Ice cream for breakfast?"

"Nope," Sophie said, a little too loud.

"You need to get laid."

"Lu, you're bad."

"Thank you," Lu said. "But seriously Sophie, what are we going to do with you? You have no idea who you are. Okay. Dinner tonight. We'll ask Olivia."

"Ask Olivia what?" Olivia said, hugged Sophie hello.

"We're taking Sophie to dinner tonight. Intervention. She needs to lay off the ice cream and find a lover. The Pub, six-thirty."

"Can we go to the new place on Main instead?" Olivia asked.

"Forgot, darling, sorry. The new place it is."

"Thank you. I'm in!" Olivia said.

She'd miss sunset with Alex. Yes. Exactly what she needed. To not see him. To not smell him. To not feel him.

To not want him.

Chapter Thirty-two

Alex

Last night left him a bit unsettled, confused. Sophie'd been on his mind when he fell asleep. Her face, the first image when he'd opened his eyes. She was so special. Truly. His heart felt warm when he thought about her. Sophie was his friend. He'd never had a friend like her. Not even Mattie. Well, Mattie'd been his love, his life, his everything. But Sophie... there was something about her that made him want more. More time with her. Alone. Talking, holding her hand, listening to her voice, sharing ice cream. He chuckled when he thought how she called a pint of Chocolate Peanut Butter her boyfriend.

He jumped out of bed, ready for his run, ready to touch her hand as he ran past her, her curvaceous body swaying to some song or another, her face focused on a book she was listening to. The woman could read.

He didn't see her on his run. Had she taken a different route? She usually walked for an hour, then headed to yoga. Today was Friday. Friday meant yoga with Lu and Olivia. They made quite a trio. Olivia loved Sophie. Talked about her, about what the three Musketeers did together. He'd called them that one day and it stuck. He loved to hear how Lu teased Sophie, how Sophie blushed. His favorite story was the one about the guy at the sushi place who'd spent the entire evening trying to make conversation with Sophie. Good looking, Olivia said, tried so hard to get Sophie to notice him. She'd chatted with him, included him in the conversation with Lu and Olivia, never realized he'd been hitting on her. The whole restaurant watched to see if it was going to happen. Sophie had been shocked when Lu told her in the car. She didn't believe her. Didn't believe Olivia. She was something. He couldn't wait until the end of the day, when he would find her sipping her pink bubbly.

Alex had a busy day. Finished a table, delivered a pair of rocking chairs to clients at a nearby town. Tried hard to work away any thoughts of Sophie.

Sophie's car was not in the driveway when he returned in the early afternoon. Bon Jovi blasting in his ears, he sanded, primed a mahogany table, eager to work away the image of Sophie's face. Muscles aching, he checked the time. He needed to shower now if he was going to make sunset with Sophie. Sophie, he thought of her eyes, her smile, her voice.

The hot water washed the stiffness of work away. His body responded to the vision of Sophie that danced in his head. He opened his eyes, pushed away the image, pushed away the feelings. Friends. That was all. Friends. Why then did her curves haunt his sleep? A one night stand. That would take the longing away, the need to release this pressure building inside. After sunset with Sophie he'd go to the Pub, find a tourist in search of fun. Fun he could do. Fun he needed.

Alex grabbed his glass of wine, walked out the back door. Took a few steps. Hmm. Sophie's house was dark, no light on the porch. He walked around the front. Her car still not in the driveway. Where was she? Where had she been all day? She'd not told him she had plans, or had she? Hmmm.

Alex dialed Olivia's number on his cell.

"Alex," his daughter answered. Noisy background.

"Is this a bad time? You on a date?"

"No. But I'm out."

"Ah, okay. What're you doing?"

"I'm out with Sophie and Lu. Intervention. Lu and I plan to get Sophie a little sex tonight."

Alex frowned. Sophie with another man?

"Does she want that?"

"She doesn't know that she wants that, so Lu and I are going to find her a man. A young man."

"Where are you guys?"

"Why?"

"Just curious."

"You're not going to show up, Alex. You're not going to come and scare the guys away. Hey, I may even find one myself."

"Don't tell me that, Olivia."

"Alex, I'm not a baby anymore. I'm a woman."

"All of twenty-four, I know."

"Here they are! Wow, Sophie looks gorgeous. And Lu... stunning, just stunning."

"Olivia."

"Bye Alex!"

Line went dead. What the hell? Sophie was out? Looking gorgeous? Alex stormed back into his cottage, dropped the wine on the counter, grabbed his car keys, marched out the front door.

Alex knew where they were. He just knew. Took the first parking spot he found when he got to Main Street. He'd find them, didn't know why but he had to. He walked a block, two, nothing. He skipped the Pub, knew Olivia hated going there. Why, he didn't understand, but now he had to find them. He peeked in Sophie's favorite Italian restaurant, looked in the diner, the Café. Walked on. One more place to look. The trendy new Restaurant/Bar with the big window, back patio with fairy lights. Sophie loved fairy lights. It was hopping tonight. People spilled out onto the sidewalk, waited for a table. Were they there? He scanned the crowd, his heart stopped. Sophie by the window. Gorgeous in pink and gold. Eyes sparkled with laughter. He could not take his eyes off her face. Shook his head, took a step forward, froze. Lu, Olivia. Benjamin. Young Benjamin who'd patted his thigh for her to sit. Young Benjamin who wanted Sophie, whispered something in her ear. She blushed. No. Not Big Ben, Sophie, not him. Alex had joked to her about him, told her she should have a fling with him, but he hadn't meant it. He didn't want it to happen. He wanted her, sitting on the porch, watching the sunset, eating ice cream. With him. Not with Benjamin. Not in bed with Benjamin. Not in Benjamin's arms. In his.

He marched into the restaurant, past the people who waited, went straight to the bar, ordered a shot of tequila. All the time his eyes on Benjamin, who showed the group something on his arm. A tattoo. Sophie ran her finger on the image. Alex couldn't tell what it was, didn't care what it was. He cared that Sophie touched him. He downed the shot, sprinted up, but came to a full stop. Lu blocked his way.

"What are you doing here, Alex?"

"Lu, what a surprise."

"Like you didn't know."

"What are you doing here?"

"You know what I'm doing here. You know what we're doing here. Olivia told me you called. What's up, Alex? Every time we take Sophie out you manage to join us. Why? Is there something we should know?"

"Don't know what you're talking about. Just wanted to get out. Have a few drinks, some food, maybe find some company."

"Ah, so you're looking for someone tonight then?"

"No, I mean, maybe."

"Good. Enjoy."

Lu looked at Alex, did not get out of his way.

"Just want to say hi. To Olivia."

"To Sophie," Lu said. "She missed sunset today. If things go the way Olivia and I planned, she'll miss sunset many days."

Lu saw the change in Alex's face.

"What's up with you and Sophie? You like her?"

"Of course I like her, Lu. She's my neighbor. My friend. You know I like her."

"Oh, I know you like her, but do you?"

Chapter Thirty-three

Sophie

Benjamin exuded sexuality. He made her a little nervous. He'd whispered in her ear how he'd created a new design for her, special, only for her, how he wanted to paint it on her skin. His voice suggested pleasure, she'd shivered. Could this gorgeous man really want her? Sex. Wow. She could not remember the last time she'd had sex. That was a lie. She could remember, not like Alex remembered to the day, but she knew it'd been five years. What was Alex doing in her head? Benjamin was there. He wanted her. Could she go through with it?

"Sophie," Benjamin whispered. "What do you think?"

Sophie could not think with Benjamin's breath on her neck. Olivia and Lu had left her alone with him. She looked over to the bar. They'd gone to get drinks. Spotted them talking to Alex. Alex? What was he doing here? Ah.

She knew what he was doing here. At the bar. He wanted someone for the night. He'd told her that's what he did when he needed to blow off steam. Glad she'd missed sunset. He would've have missed it, too. Today he hadn't wanted her friendship. He wanted sex. Maybe she did, too. Maybe with Benjamin. One time with Benjamin would quench her desire for someone else. Maybe. But what would happen after? She'd run into the young tattoo artist over and over again because it was a small town and she wasn't Lu. She'd never be as cool as Lu. Lu was Lu. An original.

"Hey, Sophe, Benjamin," Alex said, took the last step to the table, followed by a fuming Lu.

"Look what the cat dragged in," Lu said.

"Alex, hi," Sophie said, a little embarrassed. Had he seen? Did he know Benjamin wanted her? Did he know she was considering taking him up on the offer? Now it was awkward. With Alex here it was weird.

"You missed sunset," Alex said, serious, grabbed a chair from a nearby table, settled next to Sophie.

"Alex, this is a table for four, no room for you, my friend," Lu said.

Alex slipped his chair closer to Sophie's, their legs and shoulders almost touched.

"Plenty of room for you and Olivia," Alex said.

Chapter Thirty-four

Alex

"Sunset?" Benjamin asked. "You didn't miss sunset, Sophie."

She'd missed sunset with him, damn Benjamin. Damn Lu.

Sophie smiled, nervous, looked to Benjamin, then to Alex. "No, no."

"She did," Alex inched his chair closer to Sophie's. Benjamin mirrored the move.

The waitress arrived at the table with appetizers.

"Oh, five of you. Would you like a menu?" she said to Alex.

"He's not staying," Lu said, looked directly into Alex's eyes.

"I'd like the steak, medium rare, baked potato, asparagus and a glass of your house Pinot, unless someone else wants red then we can order a bottle."

"No bottle," Lu said.

Waitress nodded, walked away.

Alex caught Benjamin's look to Lu, question on his face. Damn him and his desire for Sophie. *He's not right for her*, Alex thought. Sophie needed someone different. Someone better. Someone older.

"How old are you, Benjamin?" Alex asked.

"Young enough to be your son," Benjamin gave him an aggressive look, his arm raised on to the back of Sophie's chair, his hand touched the skin on her neck.

"You mean Sophie's son?" Alex asked, smug.

"Old enough to be Sophie's lover," Benjamin flexed his biceps, looked straight at Alex. Fucking child would not get the best of him.

"I disagree. She needs someone different. Older. Smarter."

"Smarter than a man with a Masters in Business from Oxford?" Benjamin put on his most posh English accent. Irritated Alex to no end.

"So smart that he inks people's skin with that degree?"

"Smart enough to acknowledge the heart of an artist and the brain of a suma cum laude, old man."

"Hey, hey, stop it, you two," Olivia said.

"What?" Both men responded in unison, fixated on each other.

"Excuse me, ladies room," Sophie squeezed out of her chair, walked away followed by Lu. Alex and

Benjamin, aggressive eye to eye, barely noticed the object of their desire had walked away.

Chapter Thirty-five

Sophie

"What the hell is going on out there?" Sophie stormed into the bathroom of the restaurant, confused. Lu followed, amused expression on her face.

"Wow, you're swearing. Hell's frozen over or you have two dicks marking their territory," Lu said.

"What are you talking about?"

"Alex. Benjamin. Both of them want you."

"You're crazy."

"You don't think that's true? Benjamin's been flirting with you all night."

"Yeah, well, I guess he kinda likes me."

"Kinda? Sophie, he'd take you home right now if you'd let him. Serve Alex right if you left. Hey, here's an idea. Slip out. I'll tell Big Ben you're waiting for him outside. Have yourself some sexy-time girl. It's time."

"What? No, I can't do that."

"Why?"

"He's thirty years old that's why."

"No one's saying you have to marry him, just fuck him."

"Lu!"

"C'mon, say the words, Sophe... say, I want Benjamin to fuck me. Fuck me blind, deaf and dumb."

Chapter Thirty-six

Alex

Something had to give. This was not working. Sophie made her way back, not amused, Lu looked positively thrilled by their caveman behavior. Ben was not backing down.

"I think I want a tattoo," Alex said, took the chair next to Benjamin, left his open for Sophie to take. "What do you think of this?" Alex looked through his pictures, tried to find something appropriate.

"Didn't peg you for the tattoo kind," Benjamin said, annoyance in his voice when he saw Sophie sit in Alex's chair.

"There's much more to me than meets the eye."

"So, what will it be?"

"Alex! You really want a tattoo?" Olivia asked, surprised.

"I'm thinking about it, yes."

"What do you want?" Olivia said.

"Something..." Alex, pretended to look for the right word, when he was in fact trying to come up with something. He had nothing.

"A giant asshole," Benjamin said. Lu laughed. Sophie's eyes were big, alarmed, looked from one to the other.

"Is that your new tattoo? The one you were showing Sophie when I came in?"

The waitress, with impeccable timing, chose this particular moment to bring the entrees.

Chapter Thirty-seven

Sophie

Alex inched his chair closer to Sophie, offered her a chunk of his steak. He always offered her some of his food. She loved that about him. She didn't have to ask for a taste, he shared. Benjamin glared at Alex. What the hell was wrong with these guys? And what was wrong with Alex? They were just friends. What did he care if she had a fling with Big Ben? He had flings with women, as a matter of fact she was sure tonight he was going to go in search of someone. She'd noticed his restlessness the last couple of days. She knew he needed to let off steam. So did she. This closeness with Alex was not good for her. Too much. Too good. Too dangerous. But Benjamin... what could be the harm? A fling would be good for her. For her self-esteem, which was a little bit damaged because of the new wrinkles she'd discovered on her face. Well, wrinkles were the map to her life, and she was proud of that life.

"Hey, Sophe," Alex whispered, turning his back to Benjamin, blocking her from looking at the young man. "Good steak?"

"What?" Sophie said, shaking her thoughts and bringing her focus to Alex, her fork absentmindedly gathering a mouthful of pasta Bolognese.

"The steak. Good?"

"Oh, yes, thank you."

"Can I have some of your pasta?" He said, placed his hand on her forked one, turned it towards his mouth, eyes on her eyes. This did something to her stomach, the way he looked at her. She swallowed.

"Yum," he said.

Chapter Thirty-eight

Lu and Olivia

"What the hell is that? What's gotten into Alex?" Olivia said, entered the bathroom.

"What do you think?" Lu asked.

"I-I think he's into Sophie."

"Damn straight. One little problem, though."

"He has no idea." Olivia said.

"How fun is it to watch them both? The battle of the dicks. I know for a fact how big one of them is."

"Lu! I don't want to discuss the size of my father's penis."

"I wasn't talking about your father's penis. However, Benjamin's is a work of art."

Sophie barged into the bathroom, agitated.

"What the hell, you two? You left me all alone out there." Sophie said.

"She's upset. She's been swearing all night." Lu said.

"I see. Why do you think, Lu?" Olivia said.

"Hey, hey, I'm right here." Sophie said. "I don't understand what's going on out there."

"Another one that's clueless," Lu said.

Chapter Thirty-nine

Alex

Benjamin and Alex were alone at the table. Sophie followed the girls the minute Alex had taken a forkful of her pasta. She'd yanked her hand away from his, eyes wide, eyes that unsettled him. Why?

"What the fuck is wrong with you, man? What's your deal with Sophie? You guys are just friends, right?" Benjamin asked, aggressive.

"Yes, Sophie and I are friends," Alex said.

"You sure about that? 'Cause from where I'm sitting it feels like there's more between you."

Alex stared at Benjamin, said nothing.

"You blind, man? The way she looks at you, God, I wish she'd look at me like that," Benjamin said.

"What the hell are you talking about?" Alex asked.

"Fuck, you're a moron, too."

Alex fisted his hands, Benjamin chuckled. "But you should know, if Sophie ever looks at me even a tiny little bit like she looks at you, she's mine," dead serious.

Sophie, Lu and Olivia arrived at the table.

"You two are ridiculous," Lu said.

Alex jumped up, pulled Sophie's chair out for her to sit.

"I'm leaving," Sophie said. "Enjoy the rest of the evening," grabbed her jacket, purse, turned towards the exit. Alex grabbed his coat, threw money on the table, followed Sophie out.

"Hey, Sophe, wait for me," Alex said. She didn't.

"Sophie," he caught her outside the door of the restaurant.

"What are you doing here, Alex? I mean, I thought you were going to find someone to spend the next few days with. Why?"

"Why what?" Alex asked, grabbed her arm.

"You know what I mean," Sophie said, annoyed.

"Walking you home. Didn't want you to go alone."

"I wouldn't have."

Cold tightened around his gut.

"Benjamin," he said.

"No. Yes. Maybe. What the hell Alex? What's wrong with you?"

Something was wrong with him. And something was right. Sophie walked next to him, not next to Benjamin. That was right.

Chapter Forty

Alex

He'd left Sophie at her cottage. She was pissed. Didn't want to sit with him, just walked in the door, nodded, left him standing. He smiled. Didn't care she was annoyed. She was home. Alone. That was okay by him. He turned, walked towards his cottage, remembered his car was parked four blocks away. Good. Needed the walk, the air to settle his nerves. What the hell?

Instead of heading back home right away, Alex ducked into the Pub, compelled to let off steam.

"Liam," Alex planted on a stool at the bar. The last one available.

"Looking for company?" Liam asked.

"Maybe," Alex said.

Chapter Forty-one

Sophie

"So... Lu, you stayed a couple of extra days in Portland."

"I did," Lu said, looked through a display case in Sophie's art room filled with handmade jewelry. Sophie's creations. "These are exquisite," Lou picked up a pair of emerald green earrings, tried them on. Sketches on the walls mingled with watercolors and acrylics depicting ocean scenes, hearts, dragonflies, flowers. The walls, a soft blush pink, huge windows let in the light, framed views of the ocean, of the blooming garden. Sophie's worktable sported hand-blown beads, Swarovski crystals, gems, tools, sketches. A laptop computer sat on a desk under a corkboard, messy, filled with color, pictures, inspiration.

"And his name is?" Sophie asked.

"Ian," Lu said.

"And..."

"And nothing." She took the earrings off, set them aside, moved to a necklace with a small starfish encrusted with chips of diamonds. "Sophie, I want this."

Sophie took the necklace, opened the clasp, put it around Lu's neck.

"You going to see him again?"

"Who?" Lu asked, touched the charm around her neck, looked in the mirror.

"Really?"

"He's gone back to Ireland," Lu whispered.

Interesting. Lu'd been back for a few days and had not mentioned Ian. If Sophie hadn't asked, she'd have missed the spark dim when Lu told her he was gone.

"Sophie, these are fantastic. Remind me again why they're not in a jewelry store? And this watercolor," Lu walked up to a framed picture of a stormy sea. "Is not at an art gallery?"

"It's a hobby."

"A hobby my ass."

"You can have it if you want," Sophie nodded to the painting on the wall.

"I do."

A ding on Sophie's phone. Lu grabbed it.

"It's him. Again." Lu read the text out loud. "Sophe, please, can we talk?"

"Leave it."

"You haven't talked to him? It's been a week."

"I'm still mad at him."

"Let it go, Sophe. The man is crazy about you. Too stupid to know it, not stupid enough to realize that he can't afford to lose your friendship."

"It was terrible."

"It was fantastic. Two huge dicks fighting over you. My idea of Heaven!"

Lu swiped the screen, typed a response.

"Hey!" Sophie said, reached for the phone.

Sophie: I'm in my studio. Come up.

Ding.

Alex: On my way.

Lu gave Sophie back her phone. "Time to face the music, darling. Put your big girl panties on and talk to him. I'm taking these, too." Lu said, grabbed the emerald green earrings.

The sound of Alex's steps. Lu started to walk away. Sophie grabbed her hand. "Stay."

"*Fifona.*"

"Stay," Sophie said.

"Hey," Alex said, his body leaned against the doorframe.

"Come in, caveman," Lu said. "And you better have brought flowers. Lots of them."

"No flowers," Alex said, turned to walk away, "But I'll go get some right now. Orange roses."

"No, Alex, don't," Sophie said.

"Sophie, I'm sorry."

"You said that already," Sophie said.

"I know, but you still don't want to talk to me."

"Okay, Alex..."

"You forgive me?"

"Maybe."

"What do I have to do?"

"Just..."

"Just stop cock-blocking my girl. She has as much right as you to get some," Lu said.

"Lu!" Sophie said.

"It's true. The boy is crazy about you," Lu said.

"Which boy?" Alex asked.

Lu looked him straight in the eye. "You should know."

"Benjamin," Alex whispered.

"Okay, we'll go with that," Lu said.

"Sophie, do you want Benjamin?" Alex asked.

"What? I-I don't know. I mean, he's sweet and all, but he's too young."

"Never too young, *fifona*, but maybe you do need someone a bit older. Maybe," Lu said.

"Sophe, I don't know what happened to me that night. Just... I think he's not right for you and something in me took over. I know I over-stepped, made it uncomfortable for you. I'm sorry. Please, please, please forgive me."

"Three pleases in a row. I think he means it. So, Alex, let's negotiate a truce." Lu smiled. "You and Sophie agree not to spend every night together. Maybe go down to only two nights on her porch. That leaves you free to pursue... you know, pursue... and Sophie to spend her time pursuing as well."

"Lu, it's really not your place to decide for Sophie."

"I'm her agent. After all, I'm going to represent her art and jewelry, might as well represent her love life as well."

"Lu, it's okay. I can take it from here."

"Six nights a week," Alex said.

"How about we don't put a number on the nights? How about we play it by ear?"

"Starting tonight?" Alex said.

"Nope, Alex, she's busy tonight," Lu said.

"I am?" A look from Lu. "I am."

"Friends again?" Alex extended his hand for Sophie to shake.

"Friends," Sophie shook Alex's hand.

Chapter Forty-two

Alex

"Still not forgiven, eh?" Liam shot the ball through the hoop. One on one basketball night.

"Forgiven."

"Then why are you here, loser? Shouldn't you be eating ice cream with your girl?"

"She's not my girl," Alex dribbled the ball, aimed, missed. Sophie and Lu were going out to dinner tonight. Without him. He was restless.

"And... I win. Again. What's up, man?"

"Wanna go to the new bar in Seaside?" Alex said.

"Wanna go fishing?" Liam said.

"Yes."

Alex got home in the early hours of the morning. Both he and Liam had scored with a couple of tourists from New York. Sexy, sophisticated, assertive. It'd been an interesting night. Fun, yet unfulfilling. Interesting because he'd enjoyed the sex. Interesting because he was not satisfied. Something was missing and it bothered the hell out of him.

Chapter Forty-three

Alex

"So if we were to get married you'd be Alex Alexander," Sophie giggled, next to Alex, on her porch.

"No. You'd be Sophie Carter," Alex said, happy, relieved that she'd forgiven him, that things were back to normal. He'd have to send Lu a bottle of champagne, the good kind, to thank her for helping. She had. And now here they were. Just the two of them, exactly like he liked it.

"Not a chance. I'm older so by law you'd have to take my name."

"Never heard of that law."

"Now you know," she said.

"Do I now? 'Cause remember I used to be an attorney in my former life."

"I bet you haven't kept up with your brain now that you're all man, brawn and muscle sanding, carving, painting. Working those muscles so all the ladies ooh and ah when you walk in the pub. Don't think I haven't noticed," Sophie teased.

"You've noticed my muscles then."

Every day she noticed. Yesterday he knew she'd noticed when she'd gone to his studio, found him sanding a long, dark table, asked if she wanted to sand, taught her how. He'd wrapped his arms around her, placed his hands on hers, and they'd sanded in unison to the rhythm of the music playing in the background. Together. Sexy. Felt like forever before he broke contact, put some distance between them. Dangerous.

"No, yes, maybe and maybe the fumes of the glaze made you forget," she said, brought him back.

"Oh, I don't forget," he smirked.

"Well, it's a new law, so this is a warning about getting any ideas of marriage with me because that would be your name. Can you imagine? Alex Alexander. Sounds like a character in one of my romantic novels. Alex Alexander, swashbuckling pirate, Robin Hood of the seas."

"Always wanted to be a pirate," Alex said.

"Me too."

"So you're not against boats then?"

"I love boats."

"Whale watching?"

"Always wanted to, never done it," a sip of Prosecco.

"How about it then? Tomorrow?"

"Tomorrow?"

"We could play hooky from land," Alex said. He needed something. Away from routine. Something new. With her.

"And I can skip yoga."

"A must."

"My body won't like it but I didn't get this delicious by doing yoga alone. I did by eating pasta."

"And ice cream."

"That makes my deliciousness sweet."

Indeed. "So, adventure at sea?"

"Yes Captain Alex Alexander. Scarlett Redd at your service, two d's."

"Only two?" he winked.

"Wouldn't you like to know?" she teased.

"I would," he really really did. "But, is Miss Redd, two d's, ready for the sea?"

Alex couldn't get enough of spending time with her, now he'd snagged a whole day with her. On a boat. The two of them. Just the two of them.

"Let's ask Lu and Olivia to join us, you know, the three Musketeers?"

Like hell he wanted Olivia and Lu to come with them. He owed Lu but still not able to fully forgive both of them for meddling with Sophie's sex life. For setting her up with Benjamin. Grateful he'd gotten there on time. Lu had been so angry. Tough. Her problem. Olivia had been confused. Heck he was confused, but relieved. Sophie was his. What the hell? Sophie was not his. *Yes she is*, his heart said. Nope. Friends. Nothing but friends.

"Alex?" Sophie said.

"Oh, yeah. Let me call my buddy and see if he has room on his boat before we invite them," Alex pulled out his cell phone, dialed. "Hey, Mick, how you doin'?... Great! You got room on your boat for a couple of people tomorrow?... How many?" Shook his head no. "Oh, ok. What time?... Okay, yes, I'll take the two spots left... Perfect, dude, thanks," he hung up. "Two spots left," he said to Sophie. "You and me."

"Should we wait for another time when they can come?"

"No," he said.

Chapter Forty-four

Alex

Six-forty-five on the dot. Still a little dark outside. Alex knocked on Sophie's door. Seconds later, she opened, bundled in so many clothes her form barely discernible.

"Got enough clothes there, taco?" Alex said, smiled.

"It's cold."

It was cold, cloudy, a light drizzle fell to the ground. No sun threatened to warm their adventure.

"C'mon Scarlett two d's." Extended his hand for her to hold. She did.

"So snuggly in here," Sophie nuzzled herself in the warm passenger seat. "Delicious."

Like you, he thought.

"Have I told you my two favorite words in the English language?" she asked.

"Le me guess... ice cream."

"Close but no."

"Tell me," he started the car.

"Lovely. Delicious."

"Hmm," he said

After a few minutes Sophie asked. "We'll be okay on the boat, right?"

"I've seen rougher seas in my adventures, wench."

"Rough seas?" Sophie gulped.

"Sea sick?"

Sophie shook her head no. "Just chicken."

"I thought it was a dragonfly," he smiled, drove out of town, took the scenic route. "It'll be okay. Just a little chilly. Not windy enough for rough seas. Mick wouldn't risk it. Checked with him earlier. Relax."

It would take them a couple of hours tops to get to his buddy, a few towns North. Alex was quiet during the drive, enjoyed the warm energy, the peace he felt with her. Sophie, relaxed enough, chattered happy, filled his silence. He liked that she knew when to talk, when to share his silence. He could listen to her voice forever. She made a joke about her age, again. She did it all the time. Bugged him. If only she could see herself the way he saw her, she'd be surprised. If she only knew. Adorable. Sexy. She felt so young next to him, younger even than him. He felt old sometimes. Tired. Tired of fighting. Fighting to stay afloat since Mattie died. To stay alive. She'd been his life. They'd been so young, so in love. Together, always, Mattie used to say. Now she was gone. Eleven years, seven months, twenty-two days. He'd sworn on Mattie's grave that no one would ever take her place. No one.

"Where did you go?" Sophie asked, touched his arm.

"I'm here, Sophe."

She let go of his arm, sat back, quiet. He missed her chatter. Wanted her soothing voice to continue.

"Sophe, will Scarlett Redd let Alex Alexander see the infamous dragonfly?"

"No."

"But the dragonfly is all about new beginnings. Change. Possibilities. Adventure at sea, new possibility therefore dread pirate Alex gets to see Dragonflight."

"Alex Alexander, what is this obsession with the dragonfly?"

"Not the dragonfly, the tattoo. Sexy."

Sophie punched him.

"Ouch!"

"Oh, let me kiss it and make it better," she planted a noisy, silly kiss on his arm. His body reacted, hardened. Her mouth touched his jacket, his mind imagined her lips grazing his bare skin, up and down his arm. What the hell? These thoughts about her had to stop. Tell that to his body. And his dreams.

"So dread pirate Alexander, how long will we be at sea?"

"A long long time, Scarlett." Forever.

Chapter Forty-five

Alex

"Mate, been a while," Mick said, pulled Alex in a bear hug. "And who do we have here?"

"Mick, this is Sophie. My next door neighbor."

"Hi," Sophie smiled, extended her hand. Mick pulled her into his arms, held her a little too tight, a little too long. What the hell was wrong with all these men? They had to stop touching his Sophie.

"Okay, dude, let her go."

Mick belly-laughed, punched Alex's shoulder. "I see."

What did he see? Nothing to see.

The horn blared, "Time to get to work," Mick said. "Enjoy the ride."

Still overcast, soft winds. Sophie shivered.

"You're cold." Alex said.

"A little."

"Coffee?"

"Yes please."

Alex took her arm, led her inside to a room half-filled with people, hot drinks in hand. Alex ordered two lattes.

"I'm so excited, Alex, thanks for this."

Her smile, infectious, filled him with warmth.

They sat near the front of the cabin, Alex let her take the window seat, a young couple across from them.

"Hi," said the young woman. "I'm Hayley. This is my boyfriend, Zack."

"Sophie, Alex," Sophie said.

"Where're you two from?" Zack asked.

"Oh, we're local. You?"

"California," Hayley said.

"What are you doing all the way over here, in the cold, when you could be in sunny California?" Sophie asked.

"My mother lives in Medford," Hayley said.

"Exploring," Zack said. "We love exploring beaches along the coast."

"And taking pictures. Zack's an amazing photographer. I'm a writer. We're putting together a book."

"Awesome. Let us know when it comes out," Sophie said. Hayley and Sophie exchanged email addresses. So easy for Sophie to make friends, so open. Alex admired that in her. He, not so open. Never had been.

"My first time whale watching," Sophie said, shivered.

"My fifth," Hayley said, "I love it."

Alex threw his arm around Sophie's shoulder, brought her closer to him. His excuse, she looked cold. Sophie snuggled into him, drank her hot coffee.

"Delicious and so warm," Sophie said. *Yes*, Alex thought.

Half an hour later, Sophie and Hayley decided it was time to brave the elements, go outside, look for whales. Zach grabbed his camera, followed the ladies. The wind whirled around them, steady, bearable. Alex grabbed Sophie's gloved hand, led her to the railing of the boat, waves rocked their pace.

"This is so fun, pirate Alexander! Thank you."

"You are very welcome, Miss Redd, two d's."

"Not too many people on the boat. Didn't Mick say the tour was full?"

"There must have been some cancellations, because of the weather."

"Hmmm."

Sophie shivered. "Cold?" Alex asked.

"A little."

Alex stepped behind Sophie, put his arms around her.

"Better?" he asked, felt her body mold to his.

"Yes," she whispered, a little shaken.

A couple of gray whales made an appearance to the right of Sophie.

"Alex, look! Look! Wow! So beautiful."

Zack and Hayley rushed, landed next to Sophie. Zack snapped pictures, moved around to follow the whales' path. Hayley and Sophie beamed. Alex pulled Sophie closer, his head on her shoulder, taking in her sweet scent. God, he loved how her hair smelled, a mixture of rain and roses. Soothed his soul a little. Zack turned his camera to Sophie and Alex, took a few pictures.

"Hey, you two, look this way," Alex and Sophie smiled wide into Zack's lens. He clicked half a dozen shots. "Beautiful."

"How long have you two been married?" Hayley asked. Alex tensed, let go of Sophie's waist.

"Oh, we're not together," Sophie said.

"You're not? But-" Hayley said.

"We're just friends," Alex took a step away from Sophie, shoved his hands in his coat pocket, missed the warmth of her body against his. Just friends.

Chapter Forty-six

Sophie

She'd spent the better part of the day with Alex. On the road. On the boat. It'd been wonderful until the young couple asked how long they'd been married. He'd changed then. Nervous, withdrawn. His distance accentuated the cold she felt. Should she stay in? Miss the show? Watch it in front of the fire? He'd probably stay home, wanting to keep his distance. She was safe. She could go out. Grabbed a bottle of Prosecco. Two blankets, a pint of Carmel Cone. One spoon.

"Hey," Alex said, seated on his chair. His chair. He had a chair on her porch.

"Hey," she said.

"Was about to come get you."

She smiled, took her seat. Nervous.

"Sunrise and sunset today, Sophe."

Sophie stayed quiet. So many feelings swirled around, confused her. Unsettled her. So many.

"Ice cream?" he whispered. "One spoon?"

"We can share."

"Okay."

Sophie took a sip, put the glass down. Alex's hand landed on hers, turned it over, threaded his fingers with hers. Felt his gaze, did not turn to look at him, stayed focused on the colors of the sky. What the hell was wrong with her? His thumb drew small circles on her palm, her stomach fluttered. Nope. His startled face when the young couple asked how long they'd been together popped in her head, again. The look of panic. The distance.

"Thank you for today, Scarlett Redd, two ds," he said, soft.

"My pleasure, dread pirate Alex Alexander."

He chuckled, brought her hand to his lips, planted a soft kiss on her palm. She closed her eyes, all too aware of what his touch did to her body.

"Sophie, I mean it. Thank you."

She nodded. After a few more seconds of quiet he said, "So what next?" What did he mean 'what next'? Her body wanted a 'what next' with him, her mind fought against it. There would not be a 'what next' between them, she could not bear the way he'd looked at her on the boat, she could not be a hook-up and then a so long, no. She did not want that.

"What do you mean?" she asked.

"Another adventure. We should adventure once a month."

"Ah," she said, relieved. Or was she? Decided at that precise moment she needed to put some distance between them. So she would stop wanting him. Needed to find him a girlfriend. Maybe not a forever woman, but a just for right now, so she could breathe easy. So she could stop needing him. All of him. And maybe she should start dating. Maybe. She'd talk to Lu and Olivia about it. Maybe.

"Yes?" he picked up his glass to toast with her.

"Yes?" Distracted, then, "Yes," picked up her glass, tried to unlink her fingers from his. His grip tightened.

"To adventures," he said.

To adventures indeed.

Chapter Forty-seven

Alex

Sophie had been putting distance between them the last week or so. He could feel it. Baffled him. Why? Surely not the comment Hayley made on the boat? Sophie had dismissed it, joked about it all the way home. She'd called him Alex Alexander on the drive back. Told him she was the boss, and not to ever forget it. Made light of it. Eased his unease. They had a perfect friendship, he thought. Perfect.

They'd been sitting, quiet. Sunset done, still, he hadn't moved. Neither had she. He could tell she struggled to say something.

"Sophie," he said, soft. "Say it."

She started to speak. Stopped.

"Say it."

He heard the intake of a breath. "I think you need a girlfriend."

There it was. The wedge. But why?

"You're my girlfriend," teasing in his voice.

"I mean it."

"Sophie, you know I can't. Mattie –"

"Convenient excuse Alex Carter." Again, the wedge between them. Distance. No more Alex Alexander. Hurt him a little.

"Easier to never give of yourself again," she continued.

"What are you saying?"

"I'm saying that it's easy to say you'll never love again because you already had your great love. Don't be mad, Alex. I have to say this."

"I'm not mad. I thought you understood."

"I do. Believe me, I do. But, and consider this just for a moment please, what if another great love comes along? What then, Alex? Why can't you love twice in this lifetime?

"Because."

"Because?"

He was not going to let her corner him. No.

"So does that mean you're open for love, Scarlett?" New tactic.

"We're not talking about me."

"Ah, but we are now. Why should I be the only one we discuss today? Sophie Alexander, are you open for love?"

"Ship has sailed, my captain."

"So that's a no."

"Wayyyyy too old for love. Entering my sixth decade... soon. Done. Plus, all this deliciousness is too much for a simple mortal man." *Always deflecting with humor,* Alex thought.

"So you will not share your deliciousness with a simple mortal man?" Two can play at the game.

"I'm not sure there's a man around who could stand it. Instant heart attack, I tell you."

"Hmmm."

"And, confession."

"Confess away, m'lady." Hid a smile. Loved Sophie's confessions.

"Men my age and older want twenty-five year old babes. I think my trophy expiration date expired, what, thirty-five years ago."

"Well, then, what about a younger man?"

"Where? Where is he? Point him my way," she said.

Here, said the silent voice in his head. Nope. Someone else. Here was an amazing woman, with a body to die for. Yes, he knew her curves by heart, longed to know them by touch. Her breasts were magnificent, even though she kept them hidden, tight, bound by medieval torture machines. That's what Olivia called them. Every time he was with her he wanted to take her in his arms, hold her, mold her into him, feel her every curve, the softness of her skin. And her eyes, he could look into her eyes for days, years, get lost in her beauty. Her mouth... *Stop,* his head screamed. Friends. *Sophie's your friend. Nothing more.*

"I hear a certain Benjamin..." What the hell had he said? Not Benjamin.

"Now you're okay with Benjamin?" She asked.

No. Never. "He wanted you to sit on his lap."

Sophie giggled. "Hmmm. Maybe. Just maybe. My left boob could use a little ink. Maybe."

No. Not maybe. The correct answer is no, Sophie Alexander. No. Never.

Chapter Forty-eight

Sophie

"We need to find Alex a girlfriend," Sophie panted. Olivia had talked her into going on a hike, easy, she said, but Sophie did not agree. Olivia and Lu were too fast for her. Her legs refused to march at their speed. Olivia decided Sophie needed cardio. Cardio? Heart attack more likely. Olivia said it would help her avoid a heart attack. Sophie did not believe her.

"Did you hear me, Olivia?"

"I think it's a good idea," Lu said, exchanged a look with Olivia.

"Any ideas?" Olivia asked.

"I have one," Lu said, pointed at Sophie.

"Don't be silly. I mean someone young, someone sexy."

"Like I said," Lu pointed again.

"Stop."

"What prompted this, Sophe?" Olivia asked.

"He's been spending too much time with me. He needs a partner. A woman to share his life with and sitting with this old lady every night will not get him that. He needs to go out again. Stop eating ice cream with me."

"Every night? Alex spends every night with you?" Twinkle in Olivia's eye.

"Not like that. No. He needs a girlfriend."

"*Fifona.*"

"Ideas?"

Another look between Olivia and Lu.

"Well, I do have one," Olivia said.

"Yes? Who?" Sophie asked.

Chapter Forty-nine

Alex

Adventures. With Sophie. With her curves. He'd been imagining all sorts of things he'd like to do with her hips.

"Hey, Alex, where did you go?" Sophie's mouth spoke. He thought of his lips on that mouth. Remembered his body behind hers, arms around her, in his workshop, moving to an unexplored rhythm, one he wanted to explore. On the boat, his neck on hers, her scent intoxicating him.

"Huh?"

"On my God. Olivia's right, Romeo, you definitely need a girlfriend," Sophie handed him the pint of Chocolate Peanut Butter. "Here."

"I don't need a girlfriend. I need sex," Alex ate a spoonful, looked straight in Sophie's eyes. Sophie held his glare for a split second, trembled a little, let out a giggle.

"Don't look at me."

"And why not?"

"Well... because."

"Go on," Alex said, mood changed to mischief.

Sophie gulped, then, "Wait! I got it. Talia. Talia's perfect for you. Master yogi, you know. Imagine?" Sophie winked at him.

Alex blinked. He'd fallen into her trap. Yes, he definitely needed sex but not with Talia. Images of a certain soft woman naked had a certain part of his anatomy hard. And that woman was not Talia. He wanted to touch her. Her. This desire had been building since the moment he first laid eyes on her. A connection. He felt good, warm, safe when Sophie was near. Happy. He looked forward to running into her every morning. Anticipated the evenings on her porch, drinking wine, talking, eating ice cream. Looking at her. Feeling her energy mingle with his. Making love.

Pain settled on his chest. Fear. No. No. No. Attraction. Stronger than any he'd felt before. But no. Making love belonged to Mattie. Only Mattie. Love? When did love enter this equation? Sure he liked Sophie, but love? No. It was sex. He needed sex. His lack of sex clouded his feelings. On second thought, sex with Sophie could be dangerous. Bad idea. Very bad idea.

"C'mon, Alex. Talia's gorgeous. And sexy."

"Okay," he said, soft.

"Okay?" Sophie said, eyes a little too brilliant.

"Okay."

"So you'll go out with her?"

"Yes," he said, avoided her eyes, got up, walked away. Took the ice cream with him.

Chapter Fifty

Sophie

"Done!" Sophie said into the phone, overly cheerful.

"What?" Olivia said.

"Your dad said he'd go out with Talia."

"Did he?"

"Yes."

"How did you get him to agree?"

"I can be very persuasive," Sophie laughed a little too loud. "Okay, truth?"

"Yes."

"I have no idea what changed his mind. When I brought it up he was completely closed to the idea. Would not budge, then all of a sudden he went quiet. Very quiet. Looked at me as if he was taking me in, but maybe he looked past me, asking for permission."

"You think?"

"Or maybe he just wanted me to go away, stop annoying him."

"He adores you."

"Adores me so much, he said yes, walked away without even saying good-night."

Sophie hung up, walked to the fridge, grabbed the mini Prosecco Rose, pint of French Vanilla, walked out to the porch. The sun started to hide, sky turned all sorts of colors, she took her seat, ready for the show. Ready for Alex. Alex who was annoyed with her for pushing him into dating Talia. Alex who walked away, stayed away.

Chapter Fifty-one

Alex

So he'd done it. Asked Talia out. On his way to meet her. Anything to get Sophie's body out of his head. He'd been avoiding her, took his runs early, kept to his studio. No more sunsets. Worked with a vengeance, listened to rap, fought his need, reveled in his anger. He was angry with Sophie, angry she had forced him away, into the arms of Talia. He knew what would happen. He'd seen the way Talia looked at him, how women looked at him. All of them except for one, the only one he wanted. Irritation bubbled when he thought of Sophie's body haunting his dreams, his body, his heart. Hell no!

Gorgeous Talia. She was that. Young, ten years younger than him. Firm yoga body. Long blonde hair that curled, framed her face, accentuated her big blue eyes. But he wanted another set of eyes. Sparkly-hazel eyes, full of mischief, kindness and... sex. His body responded, he'd stayed away. Ignored her. She'd stayed away. Pissed him off how well she knew him. She'd been on her porch every night. Prosecco, ice cream in hand, one spoon. He'd seen her from his workshop. Ached to join her but hell no! Mad at her.

"Alex," Talia waved from the bar. They'd met at the restaurant by the sea for dinner. Best place in town. Food. Sex. Yes, he'd have sex with her at the end of the night. Maybe more than one night. He needed many nights to calm his anger, his all-consuming craving for her... for Sophie. What the fuck was wrong with him? He needed to erase his desire for her. Obliterate it. He hadn't even kissed her, so how could he miss her so much? Oh but he'd kissed her in his dreams. Over and over again. Every night since the last sunset together. Sophie's softness haunted him, imagined that softness in his bed, purring underneath him, wrapping her legs around him, taking him in, deep, lips devouring, desperate to not let go, to keep her with him forever. Telling him she loved him. Yes, she told him every night in his dreams. Asleep. Awake.

"Talia," he said, focused on the gorgeous woman in front of him. "You look beautiful tonight."

Chapter Fifty-two

Sophie

"Let's go out tonight," Sophie said to Lu after yoga class. Restless, she wanted to be away from home at sunset. It'd been two weeks of sunsets without Alex. Alex and Talia haunted her dreams. But she was happy about it. Yes, she was. Happy. Very. *Liar.* And now she needed a distraction. Some fun. Lu was always fun. Lu would distract her.

They walked into the café, ordered their usual.

"Sounds great. Where to?"

"The Pub. Craving fish and chips. Healthy, right?"

"As a heart attack. But yes, I could have a bit of a heart attack myself. Ian's been calling."

"Isn't he back in Ireland?"

"He's in Italy right now. Oh, to be under his hot, firm body again. And again. And again."

"So what are you going to do about it?"

"Nothing. No repeats, darling. Fling and go, that's my motto."

Olivia joined them.

"Hey yogis, what's brewing?"

"Planning an outing tonight. Wanna come?" Lu said.

"Can't. Have a date."

"Daniel?" Sophie asked.

"You know it. Third date this month. Maybe tonight..." Olivia said.

"Definitely tonight," Lu said. "Do it!"

Sophie sat there, jealous of her friends. Olivia so young, just starting her life, meeting men, unafraid. Lu, fearless, enjoying one man after another, well, maybe not like that, but uninhibited, sexy, free. And her, Sophie, a scared chicken, who'd pushed away the man she wanted because she was afraid. Oh, Lord, she was an idiot. But a safe idiot. Her heart thanked her for that. Fish and chips, a cocktail or five, in her future.

"Okay, Sophe, you and me. Tonight. Pub. A couple Irish men are bound to join us. Liam looks good."

"He's Alex's best friend," Olivia said, looked away.

"So?" Lu said, looked straight at Olivia. "You don't want him, let Sophie have him."

"What?" Sophie asked.

"Nothing," Olivia said, threw Lu a warning look, "I- I don't like Liam."

"Sure, let's go with that," Lu said.

Sophie, confused, looked at both Lu and Olivia "Anything I should know?"

"Nothing," Olivia said, once again, a little forced.

"Okay," Sophie said, "Lu, not going there, not Liam, so don't you dare try."

"So a couple of random tourists then."

"Maybe," Sophie said. And why not?

"Now shopping. You need a new dress. I need a new dress," Lu said.

She did need a new dress. A new pair of shoes.

"And sex," Lu said.

She did need it. Sex.

"Courage, *libelula*," Lu said.

Yes. Courage. She needed courage. She'd do it tonight. If a man wanted her, she'd accept. She'd go for it.

"You clean up nice, Sophie Alexander," Lu said, adding a bit more blush to Sophie's cheeks. "Okay. Open your eyes, look at this gorgeous face."

Wow, she did look good. The lavender cashmere v-neck dress she'd poured herself into after Lu forced her to get it, with the Spanx that kept all her bulges in, did wonders for her complexion. Hey eyes reflected specks of mauve, gold, silver. And her hair sparkled.

"Not going to be able to have a second helping tonight, Lu. I can barely breathe."

"But you look fabulous, darling," looped her arm around Sophie's. "We look fabulous," Lu admired her figure in the long black cashmere jumpsuit that hugged her every curve, her every angle. Sophie's emerald green earrings her only piece of jewelry. "Let's go. Irish boys await."

Chapter Fifty-three

Alex

Alex opened his eyes in his own bed. Alone. The fling with Talia was done. They'd been out five times in the span of two weeks. It'd been fun, but no help. Every time they had sex it was Sophie on his mind. Angry. Intense. Desperate sex. Talia was no fool. She'd broken up with him the night before. At the Pub. Sophie and Lu had been there. Sophie in that dress that hugged all her curves. Her exquisite breasts enticing with a hint of cleavage. All eyes had been on her. His eyes had been on her. Liam noticed. Talia noticed. Talia knew.

"Alex, don't blow it," Talia said.

"Hmmm?" Distracted with Sophie's laugh. She hadn't spotted him yet.

"Hey, hey, look at me."

"Sorry."

"What's with you and Sophie Alexander?"

"What are you talking about?"

"You. Sophie. Here. You've not been able to focus since she walked in. You talk about her all the time."

"I do not," glanced in Sophie's direction. She and Lu at the bar, a couple of guys offered them drinks. Sophie smiled, Lu accepted the drinks. The men joined them. Alex frowned.

"Hey, Alex, over here," Talia said, turned his face so he'd look at her.

"Oh, sorry, distracted a little." he said.

"So... Sophie?"

"What about Sophie?" Alex asked.

"Your face lights up, your eyes twinkle when you speak about her."

"Twinkle? I do not twinkle."

"You know what I mean."

Sophie, up, walked in their direction, spotted him, froze, turned around. He could barely tear his gaze away from her curves. Man she looked good.

"Look at you, you're drooling. You're crazy about her. I can't compete with that."

Alex opened his mouth to speak, closed it again. Sophie and Lu left the Pub, his eyes followed their exit. He let out a breath. Was he that transparent? Was it that obvious? Was it true?

"And she's crazy about you, you idiot! Did you see her eyes when she saw us?"

"I-what?"

"The Universe handed you both a gift. Don't be stupid," Talia leaned, touched his hand.

"Talia."

"We had fun, right?"

"Yes," grabbed her hand, kissed it.

"So..."

"So..." Alex said.

"Don't let her get away." She got up. Walked away.

Liam slapped a shot in front of Alex. "Listen to the woman. She knows."

Still in bed, Alex closed his eyes. He had the headache to end all headaches. Talia forced him to think about Sophie, as if he needed any help in that department. He hadn't slept a wink. He'd thought about Sophie in his arms. God he wanted her. Maybe if they had sex, just once, the fire in his belly would fizzle. Maybe.

He looked at his phone, six-thirty. He had half an hour to catch her on her walk. No more avoiding her. He needed to kiss his desire for her out of his system, had to get her in bed. His bed, then the itch would stop itching. Again with the thoughts, he'd already decided. But... did she want him? Yes, yes she did. Her eyes told him last night. Her eyes told him every night.

He walked out his door at six-fifty-eight on the dot. Headache eased on account of the three painkillers he'd downed with a full glass of water. Felt her before he saw her. Ear buds in, she swayed down the steps, keeping the rhythm of the sound in her ears, away from him. He stood there for a full minute, took her in, heart beating fast, then a slow jog in her direction.

"Hey, you, what's your hurry this morning?" Alex said in her ear, slowed for a moment.

Sophie jumped.

"Alex! You scared the bejeezus out of me!"

"The bejeezus?" He laughed. "What the hell is that?"

"Oh, so now we're talking. Master Alex finished his tantrum?"

"Maybe."

"Maybe?"

"Depends on how nice you are to me now, Sophie."

"I'm always nice."

"And if you wear that dress you were wearing last night for me. Just for me."

"Hey, you can't say things like that to me. You have a girlfriend now, remember? And for that you should thank me."

Alex leaned in, grazed his lips on hers, lingered a moment too long.

"Thank you," he said, jogged ahead, did not wait for her reaction.

Damn the kiss felt good, but not enough. Her lips warm, surprised, he wanted to plunge deep, but would take his time. Mess with her a little. Go slow in case he chickened out.

Chapter Fifty-four

Sophie

Stunned, Sophie stared at Alex's back. Had she imagined it? Had he really kissed her? On the lips? Well, just a peck, really. Or was it? Her lips tingled. She ran her index finger over them, straightened, stepped up her pace.

She walked longer today. An hour and a half. Faster. She rounded the corner into her cottage, climbed the steps, stopped. Alex waited for her, two coffees in hand.

"Hey neighbor, want some coffee?"

"So I'm forgiven," grabbed a cup.

"Depends."

"Oh, conditional forgiveness. Let's hear it."

"I will forgive you... if you kiss me."

Sophie choked on her coffee. He laughed.

"That appealing?"

"What the hell, Alex? Are you insane?"

"I think it's valid. You pay, I forgive."

"I don't think your girlfriend would appreciate it."

"Jealous?"

"What? No!"

"Besides, you're my girlfriend, you know that," he winked.

"You're crazy."

"So... a kiss."

Sophie laughed, she could play the game. Leaned in, grabbed his cheeks, went in close, put her lips right in front of his, then at the last second, twisted his face, planted a very noisy one on his cheek.

"Cheater."

"C'mon, boyfriend, let's catch up. It's been a couple of weeks," she said diffusing with friendship, her go-to move.

"Two weeks, three days, give or take twelve hours," he said.

Her breath caught, she took one of the chairs on her front porch. Alex the other one.

"What happened with Talia? She's gorgeous, sexy and crazy about you."

"She is all that."

"So..."

"She broke up with me last night."

"What? Why?"

"There is a reason."

"What is the reason?"

"She knows she's not you."

"Well of course she's not. She's like, what, twenty years younger than me. Skinny, sexy. gorgeous, fun. Into you. Ready for anything, yoga sex. Did I say skinny? Shall I continue?"

"Like I said, she knows she's not you and at this moment all I'm focused on is kissing you."

"Alex, be serious."

"Oh but I am. Didn't you once mention you wanted a younger lover? So, what do you say, Sophie? I'm young."

"I say it's time for me to take a shower. For you to get to work. Furniture needs to be sanded."

"Coward," Alex whispered in her ear.

"Go buff something," pushed him away.

"Hmmm... I can think of - "

"Stop!" Sophie said.

Alex laughed. "Okay. Okay. But this is not over."

"Oh it so is."

Chapter Fifty-five

Sophie

"Shit," Sophie whispered. Her eyes focused on Alex's sleeping face. Fuck! Felt her cheeks color because fucked she had. All night. With Alex. Three times. Three times! Dang! Why? Why did she say yes to the dinner party? The party! For Olivia's twenty-fifth. Small, intimate dinner for five. Olivia, Daniel, Lu, Sophie, Alex. She should have insisted they go out. She moved his arm off her shoulder, slow, steady, hoped she'd not wake him. Her temples pounded. She was still stoned. He stirred. She stilled. Prayed. *God, please don't let him wake up before I get out of his room.* His house. What would they think, Olivia and Lu? Did they know? Sophie slipped off the bed, tiptoed around until she found her clothes. Where the hell were her humongous panties? She'd worn her biggest pair. On purpose. They were tangled around Alex's ankle. Should she try to retrieve them? Impossible. Maybe he wouldn't remember. Heck! She'd deny they were hers. Lu's? Not a chance. Three sizes too big. Let him think whatever.

She'd tried to stay away from Alex all night. He'd been so different since Talia had broken up with him. She'd teased him about Talia every time he got too close, hoped it pushed him away. It hadn't. He only smiled, found another way to touch her. Her hands clasped behind her, held herself a little too rigid. Lu, Olivia, Daniel, chatted away, unaware of how aware she was of Alex. Of his scent, fresh, dark, seductive. His energy reached out for hers, mingled with hers, crowded hers. Standing in her space, he participated in the conversation. A conversation she couldn't focus on. So she'd stayed quiet. Somehow his hand found its way to the palm of her hand, his thumb traced her lifeline. She stiffened, moved away, slow. His thumb followed. She unclasped her hands, grabbed her empty glass of Prosecco. His body inched closer.

"Be back. You're out of bubbly. Gonna go get another bottle," Sophie said, stepped away.

"Want some company?" Alex whispered in her ear.

"No! No. You stay here. You have company."

"Olivia's here."

"And it's her birthday. So stay. I'll be fine going next door by myself so thank you very much."

"You're welcome very much," Alex said, running his thumb down her arm, planting a soft kiss on her neck. Sophie melted, stepped away, a little too fast.

"Hey, Sophe, where're you off to? Gummies are almost here," Lu said.

"Out of Prosecco. Be right back."

"Coming with," Lu said.

"Yes please."

Alex, the lout, laughed out loud.

"Thought you didn't need any company."

Sophie shook her head, walked out of Alex's house followed by Lu. Sophie double-stepped it through the back yard towards her cottage.

"Hey, what's up with you and Alex?" Lu opened the door to Sophie's cottage. "You holding back info?"

"I have no idea what you're talking about."

Sophie closed the door behind them, headed for the kitchen.

"He can't keep his hands off you. Always by you, whispers in your ear and you're spooked. Why?"

"I'm not."

Lu raised an eyebrow.

"Okay, yes, I've no idea what's gotten into him. He avoided me for weeks. He'd been so angry with me. Every time I tried to talk to him, he'd look past me, said nothing was wrong. And then, all of a sudden, he changed."

"Changed? How? And why haven't you said anything about it?"

"So out of the blue, after weeks of avoiding me, going on his run two hours early so he'd not run into me, a couple of days ago, he pops up behind me, grazes my lips with his, tells me he and Talia are done."

"She's not right for him."

"Why?"

"You have to ask?" Lu said, grabbed a bottle from the fridge. "Talia's not you, darling. Grow a pair."

And apparently she had. Panties left behind, Sophie slipped out of Alex's room.

Chapter Fifty-six

Alex

Alex heard a noise, did not open his yes. The heat of the night before had his body stirring, wanting more. Wow! It had been amazing. The feel of Sophie's silky skin, soft curves, the fullness of her breasts in his mouth, her legs wrapped around his waist, moaning. Her mouth on his. Man could that woman kiss. The taste of her lips had him dizzy. The memory of his tongue on the famous dragonfly, left him wanting more. And more.

"And here it is. Hello, lady dragonfly. At last we meet," he'd said, grazing her skin.

She'd laughed, turned her head, whispered, "So?"

"I like." Another kiss.

Last night he couldn't get enough of her. This morning he wanted more. He opened his eyes, expecting to see her asleep, next to him but she was gone. Her clothes were gone. Well, not all of her clothes. His bed still warm from the heat of her body. Her scent permeated his pores, the ice over his heart melted away.

He walked up to her back door. Knew she was in the kitchen, saw her silhouette through the window. His body craved her. Damn. More. Again. All of her. He'd texted. Called. She hadn't responded. To test the waters, he dialed her number. Her phone buzzed. She hadn't answered it.

He knocked, saw her stiffen, take in a breath.

"I know you're in there."

Nothing.

"I can see you."

Still nothing.

"Sophie."

She released the breath.

"Yes?"

"Open the door."

She walked to the door, did not open it.

"Alex, can we please not do this now?"

"Do what?"

Sophie sighed.

"When then?" He asked, disappointed. He wanted to take her in his arms. Kiss her. Carry her to her room, make love to her again. Make love. Not fuck. Something tugged at his heart, he stiffened. "When?" He repeated.

"Never," she whispered.

That fired him up. "Sophie," he said, harsh.

"Can we pretend nothing happened? Hey, we both had too much to drink. Plus the gummies. Can we just forget it? And you, my friend, don't like to talk about things with women. This woman is very okay with that. Glad to never mention it again."

"Sophie, please."

"I'm embarrassed, Alex. Go."

What the hell? Had she said embarrassed? What was wrong with her?

"Embarrassed? Why?"

"You know why."

"Sophie, do you regret what happened between us?"

"No, Alex, no, but, oh, it shouldn't have happened. It's going to change everything."

"Open the door, Sophie."

"No."

"Oh, so now you're the one having a temper tantrum," he turned, stormed away from her door only to turn right back. No knock, his hand went straight for the doorknob, it turned. He entered. Sophie, stood by the kitchen island, looked up when she heard the door. Took a step back.

"Alex."

"Oh no you don't, Sophie Alexander. You do not lock me out. You and I are doing this. We're having this conversation."

She opened her mouth to say something. No words came. He stood there, looking at her, wanting her.

"Okay," she said at last. "Say what you need to say."

"Last night was -"

"A mistake, I know."

He stared.

"We had too much to drink," she said.

"I wasn't drunk."

"Alex, you're off the hook. Not going to rope you into a relationship. You have nothing to worry about. We're good."

"I was going to say last night was amazing," he said, soft.

Sophie looked at Alex, eyes filled with tears. She took a deep breath, swallowed the unshed tears, stepped toward him.

"It's okay. Nobody needs to know. Your vow is safe with me."

"My vow? What the hell are you talking about?"

"You know. Mattie. You. Never again. And Alex, I can't do the hook up thing. Not with you. I like you too much. I value you too much. Our-our friendship means the world to me. Can't risk, you know..." Sophie said, eyes filled again.

Fuck, he thought. Mattie. This was all about what he'd said to Sophie months ago. That his heart was closed for business. Mattie took it with her. Never to return. His body he would share, for a short period of time, his heart, his soul, that part of his life was over. Damn this woman. Sophie knew how to listen, how to dissect his words, his emotions.

"Sophie, you were there last night. In my arms. You felt. You saw. You know," Alex took her hand, placed it over his heart. A tear spilled, Sophie looked down. He lifted her chin, forced her eyes to look at his.

"Alex, I can't," she whispered.

"Why? I'm not asking for everything. I-I just want to be with you. Again. And again. And again."

"Alex, no."

"Why?"

"You're this beautiful man. First of all, you're too young for me. And don't you dare say that age is just a number. It's not just a number to me. You're important to me. Very. You get me and I understand you. Always have. I know about your love for Mattie. Granted, I always thought it was an excuse for you to keep your heart safe. If you didn't fall in love, you would not hurt again. I get that. I respect that."

"Then why did you push me to go out with Talia?"

"Because."

"Because you thought you'd be safe if I did? If I was involved with someone else, then you, Sophie Alexander, would have an excuse not to feel."

"Alex, look at me."

"I see you, Sophie. Always have. You're the one who does not see. I wish you could just once see yourself through my eyes."

Another tear.

"I see this amazing woman, filled with love to give to everybody, but so afraid to take. A woman through and through. Breathtakingly beautiful. Funny, smart, sensual, sexy, deliciously soft, round in all the right places. And no, you and me are not a ten, me being the one, you the zero."

Sophie's eyes widened.

"I pay attention, too."

She nodded.

"I remember when you joked about that. It upset me. You always make fun of the way you look. I know, you say it first so it won't hurt. But you could not be more wrong. I'd say you're a heart, I'm an arrow. Sophie, you are by far the sexiest woman I know. Man, I've been dreaming about you, about your body, about kissing you senseless from the moment I met you. Your voice breaks me. Your eyes melt me. Your heart destroys me. I only know I want you."

"But you don't do relationships."

"It doesn't have to be a relationship. Friends. With benefits."

"Best way to ruin a friendship, sex added to the equation," she whispered.

"Doesn't have to."

"I need to think, Alex. Give me some time."

He took a step towards her, hoped to get her in his arms. She took a step back, the kitchen island a barrier between them.

"No, Alex," Sophie said.

He said nothing, his heart thumping hard in his chest, afraid.

"Please. I need time," she begged.

He nodded.

Chapter Fifty-seven

Sophie

Annie had a sign. 'Sophie Alexander', pink glitter, suns, rainbows, dragonflies, ice cream, a bottle of pink Prosecco. Sophie let go of the breath she'd been holding since Alex left her kitchen three days before. She'd asked for time. He'd given her two days, then he started texting. Not enough, she'd thought, booked a flight to see Annie. Oh how she'd missed Annie. Her understanding. Her friendship. Her love.

"So you slept with the big bad wolf and now you've come to mama to lick your wounds."

Tears streamed down Sophie's face.

"Hey, hey," Annie said, took Sophie in her arms. "It's okay. C'mon, let's go." She grabbed Sophie's hand, pulled her into the muggy heat of the Florida afternoon. "We need a cocktail, chicken wings and fried Oreos. I know a place."

"Not really hungry."

"You will be when you see where I'm taking you."

Forty-five minutes later, seated at a restaurant overlooking the water, Sophie finally relaxed.

"Okay, tell me. What did the jerk do? He dumped you after he got what he wanted? I'll kill him!" Annie said.

"No. No, Annie. He didn't. He wanted more. I- I just couldn't. You know, he's gorgeous, and younger and I'm -"

"Wait a minute Sophie Elizabeth Alexander. You're telling me the man wants you and you walked away."

"Yes."

"Why are you such a doofus? What's the matter with you? Why are you here? And why are you crying?"

"He saw me naked," more tears.

Annie let out a laugh, which had the people at the next table turn to look at them.

"Of course he saw you naked. You had sex," Annie whispered.

"I know," Sophie whispered back.

"Is this why you're so upset?'

"No, well, one of the reasons. But no. It's just, I like him, Annie. I really really like him and this is going to ruin everything."

"Why?"

"Because he only does hooks up. He doesn't want a relationship."

"Do you?"

"I-oh, I never thought that would ever come up again in this lifetime. You know I didn't, but there's something about him. I kind of need him in my life, and sex just messes things up. He never stays with anyone for long. He'll never commit."

"How do you know?"

"He told me. From day one I knew. I believed him. And I..."

Sophie's phone rang. Alex. She let it go to voicemail.

"How many times has he called today?" Annie asked.

"Seven."

"Texts?"

"A whole bunch."

"Have you answered?"

"I asked him to give me time."

"What the hell, Sophie? What's wrong with you?"

"I don't know. I'm just so confused."

"Was it terrible?"

Her phone dinged, indicating a voicemail. A moment later, a text came through. Annie grabbed the phone, read. "Sophie, please, don't shut me out. Where are you? Please talk to me."

"Sophe," Annie said.

"Oh, Annie, it was wonderful. Amazing. I've never felt what I feel for him."

"So what's the problem, you crazy cat?"

"He's younger than me."

"Seven years. Pft!"

"He's my next door neighbor."

"Convenient."

"My friend."

"Good. Always good."

"He's still in love with his dead wife."

"How long has she been gone?"

Sophie knew exactly how long she'd been gone, but said simply. "Over eleven years."

"Okay. That's a problem."

Annie motioned for the waitress, ordered two more margaritas and a second order of fried Oreos. Sophie's phone dinged, again. Annie motioned for Sophie to look. Sophie shook her head. Annie read, "Your boyfriend, Mr. Chocolate Peanut Butter misses you. A lot."

Sophie attempted a weak smile.

"Funny, too," Annie said. "You gonna answer his text?"

"Not today."

Chapter Fifty-eight

Alex

Where the hell was she? Why wouldn't she answer the freaking phone? He couldn't stop thinking about her. He wanted her, all of her. The sex had been amazing between them, mind-blowing. So feminine, funny, self-deprecating. Perfect. He craved her body, her delicious body, so womanly, so soft. The scent of her skin so sweet, tasted like fresh peaches with honey. Right now he wanted to run his nose, his mouth, all over her. Smell every inch of her. Kiss, taste, touch. All of her. He wanted to be inside her. Forever. He knew she'd enjoyed it, heck, she'd purred under his touch, his lips, his teeth. Asked for more with a look, with a word. God, the things he'd done to her, she'd done to him. Their eyes locked when he was in her, moving at her rhythm, slow, hot. His rhythm, fast, hard. Their eyes open, lips touching, light, intense, left him wanting more. He could not remember the last time it'd been like this for him. And she'd just disappeared, as if it had been nothing. It had not been nothing, Sophie Alexander. It'd been something. Quite the something. Five days, fifteen hours. Where the hell was she? She'd told him she needed space. He'd given her two days. Two long, agonizing days without her voice, without her face, without her body. Damn it, he wanted more. He wanted her. Then he'd called. Voicemail. Texted. Nothing. Nothing!

"Sophie, Sophie, I - " about to say he loved her. Because, maybe, but Mattie. Guilt flooded over him. He hadn't thought of Mattie since Sophie disappeared. Not even once. Until now. "Oh God," he whispered, rubbed his temple. Maybe it was okay. Better that she was gone. Maybe.

His phone dinged. He pulled it out of his pocket. Sophie.

Sophie: Hey. Hi.

Relief. Radio silence over. Mattie flew out of his mind. He'd think about her later, right now he wanted, no, needed to talk to Sophie. He hit her contact, he had to hear her voice. Ask her a million things. Listen to a million things. Rang three times. She answered.

"Hi," she said.

"Where are you?"

"With Annie."

"Florida?"

"Yep."

"Why?"

"Oh, I don't know, Alex."

"You didn't tell me you were going."

"I know."

"Why?"

"It's what I do. I run. When something's too much for me, I run."

"And this is too much?" He was about to say us, but, no. No us for him. Us was Mattie. Only Mattie. But Sophie, oh Sophie, he ached for her.

"We're friends, Alex. What happened between us changed everything. I don't want anything to change."

"It doesn't have to."

"Doesn't it, though? Hasn't it already?"

Maybe. Maybe it had but he didn't care. He wanted her. With him, like he hadn't wanted anybody in a very long time.

"Okay, yes, things have changed but it can be good."

"I-we need some space. The two of us, to figure it out."

Space is definitely what he didn't need, what she didn't need.

"Sophie, come back. Please. We can work this out. Together."

She didn't respond.

"What if we promise we'll remain friends, no matter what?" He said.

"I'd like that," she whispered.

"So done. But we can't deny the attraction between us, Sophe. I think about you all the time. I want you all the time."

"Alex, I- I'm nervous about this."

"Scared little *fifona*?"

Sophie laughed. "Yes."

"How about we come up with a plan that works for both of us?"

"Ground rules?"

"Yes, if that's what you want."

"Okay."

Relief.

"When will you be back then?" Hoped she'd say today.

"Next week. Wednesday maybe."

Next week? Wednesday? That'd be another seven days without her. Not acceptable.

"How about tomorrow?"

She laughed. Oh that laugh, went straight to his center. He hardened.

"Alex, Annie and I have plans for the week."

"Plans can change. Friday?"

"Tuesday."

Not good enough. "Saturday?"

"Monday."

"Sunday, final offer," he said. Statement. The way her voice said each day got to his heart. She negotiated. No way in hell he'd wait a week for her. He'd fly to Florida if she didn't agree to Sunday.

"Sunday, okay" she said. "Ground rules. You come up with one. I come up with one. We text, accept. Okay? Oh, and the vow... I already know that one. But it should be the first one on your list."

Closed his eyes. Damn this woman. She knew him.

"Okay," he said. "No Benjamin. That's the first one on your list."

"Benjamin? What does he have to do with this?"

"I-I just, no Benjamin, okay?"

"Okay."

Chapter Fifty-nine

Sophie

Sophie and Annie lounged by the pool, tropical drink, little umbrella.

"This is the life," Annie said.

"Never pegged you for a slug."

"You're the slug."

"I know. Is it wrong that I'm loving just doing nothing with you?"

"And you're putting off going to see your hunka hunka man as long as you can?" Annie teased.

"He saw me naked!" Sophie made a face.

"What are you, twelve?"

"Chubby, that's what I am."

"Oh, Sophie, you are so naive."

Ding. Text.

"The lone wolf is lonely," Annie said. "And he doesn't care if you're chubby. I bet he wants to see you naked again, and again," Annie winked.

"Stop!"

Sophie blushed, read.

Alex: So... coming home tomorrow, right?

Smile.

Sophie: Today is Thursday. Tomorrow is Friday. I'm going back on Monday.

Alex: Nope. Tomorrow.

Sophie: Okay. Sunday then.

Alex: New rule. Re-arranging the days of the week. Sunday comes after Thursday.

Sophie: Leave me alone. Eating fried Oreos and crab legs.

Alex: Happy to fry a few Oreos here. Wink emoji.

Sophie showed the text to Annie.

Sophie: I'm being the perfect slug. Swimming pool. Hammock. Tropical drink with umbrella and everything. Cabana boy.

Alex: Rule number twelve... no cabana boys.

Sophie: Crazy face emoji.

Alex: U in a bikini? Pic please.

Sophie: No bikini.

Alex: Pic please.

Sophie: Use your imagination.

Alex: U naked? Cause that's what I'm imagining.

Sophie blushed.

"Oh my God, you're sexting!!" Annie screamed laughing.

"I am not!"

Alex: Picture please.

Sophie: Gotta go. Jumping in pool.

Alex: That hot?

Sophie: Bye.

"Me thinks it's time to retire the granny panties. C'mon Juliet, I know a guy," Annie winked.

"A guy or a place?" Sophie asked.

"Both."

Annie smiled, reached out for Sophie's hand, squeezed.

"You're happy," Annie said.

"I- I think I am."

Chapter Sixty

Alex

Sunday morning. Portland airport. Alex scooped Sophie into an embrace. Kissed her, relieved she was in his arms.

They'd talked everyday, set down some ground rules he could live with, she could live with. No Benjamin, until their fling was over, and then, maybe never, not even then. Nobody would know about their affair. He was not ready for that, never would be. She knew. She'd told him she understood. They were just going to have a friendship fling. "With lots of sex," he'd said. She'd agreed.

"So..." she said.

"So..." he said, started the car, kept her hand in his.

"What now?"

"Well, for starters I'm not letting you out of the bedroom for a week, maybe two."

She blushed, nervous. God, he could not wait until she was blushing under him, naked, until his mouth tasted every inch of her body.

"What about Lu? Olivia? Didn't you tell them you were coming to get me?"

"Nope. Told them you'd be back next week, to leave you in peace to spend time with Annie."

"Ah," she said. "Your rule number two in place. Our secret."

"Yes. Our secret. Not sharing you for a bit. Eight days, six hours, give or take a few minutes without you. I need the same amount of time with you. Alone."

Chapter Sixty-one

Sophie

Sophie looked into Alex's eyes. He'd pulled her into his arms the minute he'd opened the door of her cottage. Kissed her senseless. Then, he'd pulled away, a silent question in his eyes.

"Yes?" Alex asked.

"Yes," Sophie said, nervous.

Alex grabbed her hand, led her to her bedroom, slow.

"I see we got new underwear," Alex said, glint in his eye, running his finger down the lacy panties Sophie had on.

"Annie made me get them," she blushed, remembered the humongous pair she'd left behind tangled in Alex's feet.

"Does that mean the Audrey Hepburn panties are getting a well-deserved rest?"

"Audrey Hepburn?"

"The ones you left behind."

Understanding, she buried her head in his chest. "Don't remind me."

He kissed her collarbone.

"I'm gonna need those back," she said, a little out of breath from his lips.

"Not a chance."

She groaned, his tongue on her nipple, image of the panties gone, only the pleasure of his mouth remained.

Chapter Sixty-two

Sophie

She'd been back for two weeks, two weeks with Alex. Every night. Every day.

"Hey, Sophe, earth to Sophie, class is over," Lu said, poking her. "Coffee time. And dish time. Something's up. I want to know."

Sophie stretched, opened her eyes, Savasana, her favorite part of yoga, after all the sweating, the poses, the moment to relax, to not think, or relive the night before in her case, when she'd melted into Alex, screamed his name, reached heights she never knew possible. Alex, the thought of him brought a goofy smile to her lips, bedroom eyes.

"Oh, dragonfly, you're having sex! I knew it. You're so transparent."

"Shhh, be quiet Lu."

"Olivia -" Lu said.

"No, Lu, not Olivia," grabbed Lu's arm. "Please, I'll tell you, but Olivia cannot know. So shhhh..."

Lu nodded. "Understood. But you're telling me everything, you little tramp."

Olivia joined them. "Ladies, coffee?"

"Not today, honey, we can't. How about we meet at Sophie's for this amazing sunset? What do you say we crash it this evening? Not fair that Alex is the only one who gets to enjoy it with Sophie," Lu said.

Sophie looked at Lu. Lu ignored her.

"Sounds like a plan. What can I bring?"

"Something yummy, and sexy. Oysters maybe? You never know who could be in the mood for a little loving," Lu's eyes sparkled. Sophie kicked her.

Olivia laughed. "Oysters it is!"

"I'm having sex and it is awesome," Sophie said, seated on Lu's couch. Lu poured her a glass of Prosecco.

"So the big bad wolf finally admitted he had the hots for you."

"He more than admitted, Lu."

"Let me guess. The night of Olivia's party."

"How did you know?"

"Oh, darling, the man has been drooling over you since he first laid eyes on your pretty face. But something was different that night. He could not keep his eyes, his hands, his dick off you. I looked, he had a very hard hard-on every time you were anywhere near him. And he followed you like a puppy in heat."

Sophie giggled.

"Really, giggles? Tell me everything, darling. Everything. Wait, didn't you go to Florida for two weeks? Because of the sex?"

"I freaked out."

"*Fifona*! You left?"

"A couple of days later. Didn't tell him. Would not answer the phone, his texts, until..."

"Annie set you straight."

Chapter Sixty-three

Alex

Alex took a step out of his house, eager to spend a little time with Sophie. Maybe kiss, maybe feel her body, maybe take her on the chair. Chair. They needed something more comfortable out there, a daybed maybe. He heard Olivia's laugh, looked to Sophie's house. What the hell were Lu and Olivia doing on Sophie's porch, laughing, drinking, taking his place? Sunset was their time. Well, so was bedtime, morning and whenever he could get time with her. His time with her. Not ready to share her. Not yet.

"Alex," Olivia said. "We're dancing in the moonlight today. Full moon later."

They were going to stay that late? God, he'd missed her lips, all day. His lips would have to wait. He kissed his daughter's cheek, nodded at Lu, who winked at him. What the hell?

Sophie walked out of the cottage, wearing a flowy thing that hinted of what was underneath. Pink with orange flowers. A bit transparent. A certain part of his anatomy noticed. Wanted.

"Alex, look what Lu gave me? Isn't it fabulous?"

You're fabulous, he thought. "Yes."

"So this is what you two do every night," Lu said. "I think I'm going to like joining you. Often."

Not if he could help it. He loved Lu. Adored Olivia, but this was his time with Sophie. This was their thing. Wasn't ready to widen the circle. Yet. Maybe when the physical part of their relationship was done, then this foursome would be perfect. Today, he wanted just the two of them.

Sophie walked back into her cottage. "Snacks," she said.

"Let me help," he followed her in. The minute they were in the kitchen, he pulled her close. One eye on her, the other one on the door.

"Why are they here?" he asked.

"Because," she said.

His gaze on her lips.

"Careful Romeo, your daughter's outside."

"Just one kiss. Been waiting all day to kiss you," pulled her close, ran his hands down the length of her back, settled on her ass, his face inched closer.

"Hey, Sophe," Lu said from the door. Alex let go. Damn the woman and her bad timing. "Need any help? Real help?"

"We got it covered," Alex said.

"I bet you do," Lu said, walked back out.

Sophie laughed, pushed him away. "Go, I'll be right out."

"How long are they staying? Because I have plans for you."

"Plans are going to have to wait. They're staying. We're dancing. And you're dancing with us."

"I only dance with you, naked, alone," he ran a finger down her neck, on her skin, down the front of her top, inched its way until it circled her nipple, over her bra, soft, just like she liked. He knew just how she liked it.

"Stop," she shivered, her nipple pebbled.

"I can't. I want you," he whispered in her ear, his body hard. "See," brought her hand to the front of his pants for her to see how much he wanted her. How he couldn't get enough of her.

Laughter outside.

"Olivia," barely a whisper. That stopped him, brought him back to reality. He took two steps away from her.

"Guys, what's taking so long? I'm hungry," Olivia walked in the kitchen, followed by Lu. Two seconds before she would have caught him looking at Sophie, touching Sophie, wanting Sophie.

Sophie spun to open the refrigerator, looked for something. The mood changed, the space between them widened. Olivia. His daughter. Mattie's daughter. Hit him like a waterfall of ice water. Cooled the heat coursing through his body. This was the first time he'd been with Olivia and Sophie at the same time since they started having sex. He had to be careful. Olivia could never know.

Walked out of the kitchen, headed out. Home. Better to go home. Better to not be near Sophie. Better to not want Sophie. Not today.

Chapter Sixty-four

Sophie

Sophie, face in the fridge, cooled her desire. Dang, Alex could rev her up with a look, a touch. Oh, how he touched her. Sent shivers through her body. She wanted him. Bad. She more than wanted him. She cared for him. A lot. And needed him. She did.

Ding. Text.

Alex: Leaving The Three Musketeers to a night of dancing and female bonding.

"Hey, Alex's gone," Olivia said, stepped back in the kitchen.

"Yes, he just texted."

"Coward," Lu said.

Chapter Sixty-five

Alex

Uneasy, Alex paced around his cottage. Close call. Damn his desire for Sophie.

Paced into his bedroom. No Sophie tonight. Lu made it quite clear. They were staying. Late. Why was he so upset about this? It was just one night. He'd been with Sophie for fifteen nights straight since she got back from Florida. Why did it feel so heavy that she was not with him right now? What was he so afraid of? He sat on his bed, dark room lit only by the moonlight streaming from the window. Full moon tonight. Heard the echo of laughter, music, talking. Ripped his heart out to hear the voice of his daughter, happy, mingled with Sophie's. It should be Mattie's voice. Mattie laughing with Olivia, not Sophie. Mattie. Oh, Mattie. She'd been a distant memory for quite some time now. He barely remembered the sound of her voice, the silly little giggle that escaped her lips when he touched her. The blue of her eyes. He looked up, her picture on his dresser stared at him, gnawed at his heart. Guilt. Guilt that her image blurred, morphed into Sophie's. Sophie. He fisted his hand, squeezed it shut, hard. Angry. No. Alex rose, moved, slow, deliberate, shuffled to the dresser, picked up Mattie's picture. Mattie smiled, reminded him of their love, their life, their promises. He needed more of her, more Mattie. More. He walked to the closet, found his box of memories, brought it to the bed, opened it. He hadn't looked at the pictures for a while. It hurt too much. Pulled out one of his favorites, a photo of him and Mattie kissing. Their faces filled the frame. A four by six in a simple silver frame. He'd put it away years before when he needed to let go of some of the pain. Pain he'd clung to like a life boat, an oxygen tank to keep him alive, but not afloat. Half in, half out. He knew as long as he held to the memory of her, he would stay in that in-between place where the ache he felt was familiar, comfortable, comforting.

New feelings, new pain. Fear. He stared at the photograph for what seemed an eternity. He stirred, closed the box, kept the photo, placed it on his dresser. Protection. He needed protection from these new feelings that threw him out of balance. No way. This thing with Sophie needed to be light, easy. Shallow. Playful. She was so easy to be playful with, to keep it friendly. Yes. She'd said it. Friends with benefits. Emphasis on friends with lots of benefits because, like it or not, he could not get enough of her. Hearing her voice mingled with Olivia's had sobered him. He knew three things for certain. One, he could not stay away from Sophie. He wanted her. All the time. Two, the photo stayed on his dresser, where he placed it, a reminder, a layer of protection for his heart because, three, this friendship could be dangerous.

He looked at his watch. Eleven thirty. Music still wafted through his window. He shut it, undressed, slipped into bed, alone for the first time in fifteen days. Closed his eyes, pushed the image of Sophie away from his mind. Fell asleep in an instant, blessed relief for the burden that pressed on his heart.

Chapter Sixty-six

Alex

Alex opened his eyes, disoriented. Alone in his bed, the panic of the night before gone with the new day. Shook his head. Stupid thoughts. He chuckled at the intensity of his feelings the night before. Of course this thing with Sophie was nothing really, just fun. Yes he wanted her. Yes he loved spending time with her. Friendship and sex. After all her body thrilled him, left him breathless. Her smile melted him, warmed him, filled him with desire. Yes, exactly what he needed for as long as it lasted. It would fizzle out. He was sure of that. It always did but for now, he wanted her.

Chapter Sixty-seven

Sophie

Ding, text came through. Sophie opened one eye, snuggled her pillow. Still dark outside. She picked up her phone. Five-thirty. She'd stayed up past midnight dancing in the moonlight. No walk today. No yoga. Sleep. Another ding. Two messages.

Alex: Sophie

Alex: U up?

Sophie typed: no

Ding. Quick response.

Alex: U sure?

Sophie: yes

Alex: then why r u answering?

Sophie smiled, typed.

Sophie: because my phone keeps dinging

Alex: u don't have to respond

She didn't. Three dings in a row.

Alex: Sophie

Alex: I know

Alex: u're up

She waited. Two fast dings.

Alex: Sophie

Alex: u up?'

She giggled, typed her response.

Sophie: What are you, twelve?

Alex: I miss u

Sophie: You should have stayed. Danced.

Alex: u had company

Sophie: So?

Alex: haven't kissed u in hours

Sophie shivered, ran a finger on her lips, imagined his mouth on hers.

Alex: Sophie, u up?

Sophie: Would it kill YOU to spell the word YOU?

Alex: I miss

Alex: You

Alex: You

Alex: YOU

Alex: I want

Alex: YOU

Sophie shook her head. She and Alex had a pact. They'd decided to quench this thirst they had for each other physically, leave everything else out of the equation. Rules. She decided she had a secret 'fuck buddy'. Who knew she still could? But she did. And it was sexy, gorgeous, delicious Alex. He was delicious but she was going to have to keep her heart locked tight while she gave of her body. Still baffled that he could not get enough of her. How he wanted her, worshiped her body.

Alex: Sophie...

Sophie: Okay sex addict, where are you?

Alex: Outside your door.

Sophie's nipples hardened, fully awake now, she wanted him, too. She got out of bed, flew into the bathroom. Her phone dinged a few more times, she did not look, only smiled. Splashed water on her face, ruffled her hair, quick brush of her teeth. Walked to the front door, saw his reflection in the window. She stopped. Smiled. Unlocked the door, took a step back.

"Come in," she said. Alex opened the door, found Sophie standing naked, her nightgown pooled around her feet on the floor.

Chapter Sixty-eight

Sophie

Feelings. Lots of feelings bubbled inside her. For Alex. Feelings she wasn't supposed to be feeling. She'd promised. Rule number one. No relationship. Only casual sex, except that sex with Alex was anything but casual. The way he looked in her eyes when he was inside her, the way he draped his arm on her waist, pulled her back to him, held her hand, kissed it, slept with her when she stayed over at his place. At her place he slipped out at dawn. He had to leave, could not bear to stay. She'd see the guilt all over his face. Her choice to stay, his choice to go. Problem, big one, she wanted him to want to stay. That's all she could think about these days. Stay, she'd think. Stay. Two months two weeks and two days he'd been sneaking out of her room.

"Earth to Sophie," Lu said. "What planet are you on?"

Lu, Sophie and Olivia waded the tide pools at the beach.

"Look!" Olivia pointed at a beautiful starfish on a rock.

"Like my necklace," Lu pulled the piece of jewelry out of her shirt.

Sophie and Lu gathered around her.

"Wow! Amazing."

"Sophe, showed your necklace to Sandra," Lu said.

"Sandra?" Sophie asked.

"She manages the boutique by the Café. She wants to see more. Showed her the earrings as well. Told her I'd bring you by sometime," Lu said.

"That's amazing," Olivia said. "I absolutely love the bracelet you gave me for my birthday. I get so many compliments on it."

Sophie smiled. Made her happy to see friends enjoy her work. Excited her a little to think Sandra could be interested in her jewelry, that she could maybe make a career out of a hobby. A hobby she loved.

"I'm glad," Sophie looked at Olivia.

They walked to the next pool, explored, enjoyed, looked for shells.

"So, Olivia," Lu said, glanced at Sophie. "What's up with your dad?"

"Alex? Nothing, I think. I haven't seen much of him lately."

"I wonder why?" Lu said. Sophie shot her a look.

"I don't know."

"You think he has a new woman?" Lu asked.

"Nah. I think Sophie here keeps him busy not needing a new woman."

"What? I- I – we're just friends."

"Don't I know that," Olivia said. "He tells me all the time when I ask him about you."

"How long do his 'hook-ups' last?" Lu asked, eyes on Sophie.

"Not more than a couple of weeks. He's more of a three timer. I don't get it, though. My mom's been gone for so long. I'd love for him to find someone," Olivia looked straight at Sophie.

"Yes," Lu said. "That would be great. Two weeks, huh? What do you think of that, Sophe?"

She didn't. Think.

Chapter Sixty-nine

Sophie

"C'mon, Alex, we gotta get up." Alex didn't budge, legs tangled, her head on his chest, the clock ticked five thirty-five. They'd spent the afternoon in bed, new for them, always at night, at the end of the day. They'd watched Love in the Afternoon with Audrey Hepburn and Gary Cooper. Alex suggested they try this love in the afternoon thing. Sophie hadn't needed much convincing. But now it was time to go.

"Sophe, do we have to? Yoga's not my thing, you know that," his hand sent bits of electricity down her back, fingers rubbed her head, seductive.

"I do but your daughter is teaching her first night class and it's a big deal. We're going to be supportive."

"Yoga? Really? I'm not very flexible," twinkle in his eye.

"You could have fooled me," untangled her legs from his, dropped a soft kiss on his chest, started to get up.

He pulled her back, took her lips in his. "Okay, so we'll be a little late," she said, out of breath.

"How about... we apologize... tomorrow?" Between kisses.

She pulled back, placed a hand on his chest, separated them. "So that works for you, but what would my excuse be? We're not supposed to be together, remember? Don't you think it'll be a bit strange if neither one of us shows up? Especially since I confirmed this morning. Nope. Let's go, lazybones."

"Okay. But..."

"No buts. We'll take a place at the back of the class, so you're not self-conscious. You just follow my lead. I know all the moves."

"Do you now?"

"I do."

"How do I follow?"

"I know yoga, just follow my lead."

And he did.

Chapter Seventy

Alex

"Hey, Sophe," Alex whispered. "How am I supposed to bend like that, keep my legs straight?"

Sophie looked in his direction, suppressed a smile. "Hey, stiffy, bend your knees."

Did she say stiffy? Really, when he was contorted, she said stiffy? He was stiffy. For her.

"Stiffy? Really? You know what that means, right?"

The lady in front of him shushed him. Sophie giggled. God that giggle brightened his world. He lived to hear the giggle on those lips he wanted to kiss. All the time.

"Just look at me and be quiet," Sophie whispered, eyes front.

"Yoga makes you bossy. I think I like it," Alex whispered back. The lady who shushed him looked back at him. "Sorry," he mouthed.

The class continued, Alex tried, really tried, but his muscles didn't like how they needed to stay put for hours on end, well seconds really but it felt like hours to him. How Olivia had chosen a career in human torture beat him. How Lu and Sophie enjoyed this mind, body, soul bending agony was beyond him. Still, the sight of Sophie's face concentrating, her body twisting, strong, flexible brought a fire to his belly. He was going to insist on doing naked yoga at home. Downward Dog would be something to inspect from all angles. And he was going to examine every inch of the pose.

"Hey," whispered Sophie. "Look at me, switching positions."

Chapter Seventy-one

Sophie

Sophie kept her eyes on Alex, made sure he followed her lead. She'd stopped listening to the instructions Olivia gave about the new pose. Alex's contorting sexy body distracted her. She was not too familiar with this particular position, but she followed what she remembered. Lying down, she grabbed both her feet, one in each hand, lifted her legs up. Alex followed suit, winced because his flexibility, well, was not flexible enough. Sophie rocked from side to side, both feet in the air, Alex mimicked her. Sophie stifled a giggle, Alex looked like a frog and so did she. She turned her gaze to the front of the room. Everybody was doing bridge, feet planted on the ground, still, holding in place. She and Alex were doing God knows what, defective lotus flowers floating in a murky pond more like it, rocking like crying babies. Wait! That's exactly what it was. The crying baby, no, the happy baby.

A laugh escaped from her lips, disguised as a cough. Alex looked around, smiled a smile that lit up her Universe.

"I thought you knew what you were doing," he mouthed.

"Shut up," she mouthed back, giggles rocked her chest, legs still up in the air. Alex's chest shook, tried to suppress a laugh. It was over. The peace and zen of the yoga class, over. Never to return.

Chapter Seventy-two

Alex

Alex felt the shaking that came from Sophie's stomach as she pretended to cough during savasana. Her eyes closed, tears of laughter rolled down her cheeks, tummy, a bubbling volcano, fighting the need to erupt. Cough, giggle, cough. Contagious. He cleared his throat, a laugh escaped his lips, brought his mind to the present moment. He'd been imagining her doing the dreaded position in the nude. The infamous happy baby. Stiffy was not a euphemism anymore. It was his reality. He was hard for Sophie. So hard even the laughter had not stopped it. But her attempt to control the chortling made him join in her giggle, cough, giggle pattern. He felt the judgmental woman in front of him stiffen, like his stiffy. Pun intended.

"Hey," he whispered. Sophie looked at him, huge smile, tears rolling down her cheeks. Giggle, loud cough. "Is this over soon? My stomach hurts from laughing."

Chapter Seventy-three

Sophie

"Lu, I have no idea what to get Alex for his birthday." They were on their way to Sandra's boutique. Alex's birthday, two weeks away, weighed heavy on her mind. She really had no clue. She wanted to give him something special, personal but not too personal.

"Darling so simple."

"What?"

"The man is a sex-addict when it comes to you."

Sophie blushed. Lu wasn't wrong. They'd been spending every night together. Every blissful, sexy night.

"So give him, you know..." Lu said, suggestive.

"I already give him that."

"I know, get his name tattooed on your breast."

Sophie laughed out loud. Alex would not be happy if she saw Benjamin again, if she let Benjamin touch any part of her body. Rule number one for her. No Benjamin. She hadn't thought about him in a long long time.

"I don't think so."

"How about a picture of you naked."

"Really? Have you met me, Luciana? Do you know me at all?"

"I have darling, I think you have not met you. He would love that."

A picture. An idea.

Chapter Seventy-four

Alex

"Happy Birthday to me," Alex whispered in Sophie's ear, bodies tangled in an embrace, naked, on his bed. Sophie looked up to him, love in her eyes. "Happy Birthday gorgeous," she murmured on his lips. He shivered, his insides churned. Thrilled him to hold her, feel her, kiss her.

"You think I'm gorgeous."

"I do."

"Even at fifty-four?" he said. "Not so young anymore, eh Sophe."

"Hmmm. Still a young man," she shifted her body, tried to move away. He pulled her closer.

"Where do you think you're going?" he asked.

"Olivia's coming over early, remember? Birthday breakfast. You two are spending the day together."

They always did. Had their rituals for his birthday.

"Anyway, I'll see you later tonight."

"Not yet," he held her tight. "Stay a little while longer," nuzzled her neck, his hand cupped her breast, thumb ran circles on her nipple. She moaned. He knew how to get her to stay. He had tricks up his sleeve. He still had a couple of hours before Olivia showed up. He wanted them with Sophie.

Chapter Seventy-five

Sophie

Sophie wanted to stay, boy how she wanted to stay, celebrate with him, with Olivia. But she needed to go. A little space today. She'd noticed how every couple of weeks another picture of Mattie, of their life together, appeared somewhere in his house. Started after the night Olivia almost caught them in the kitchen. A small picture of Alex and Mattie kissing on his dresser. He said nothing. Sophie saw everything, said nothing. His way of reminding her, or maybe reminding himself, about their agreement, about the fact this thing between them was nothing but a fling. Casual. Last night she'd spotted a wedding photo, Mattie radiant, Alex stared adoring, on the wall in the hallway, which led to his bedroom. It hurt. She'd been thinking about how much it hurt, how she needed to start putting a little distance between them. For her sake. But maybe not today. She needed to hang on to him today, she couldn't get enough of him. Of his skin, his scent, his hands, his eyes, his laugh. His love, except, that's right, he didn't love her. He couldn't love her. He wanted her and, after all, love and want were not the same thing.

She moved, he held her tighter. "Not yet," he said. She gave into the embrace, to the physical need which lived permanent in her belly when she was next to him, when she saw him, touched him, loved him. She did. Love him.

"Wait. I need to give you something."

"I don't need anything but this right now," he said, his fingers trailed up her thigh, found the spot between her legs. "Unless you finally decided to show me what Downward Dog really looks in the light of morning... in your birthday suit," kissed the spot between her neck and shoulders. The one that gave her goosebumps. Pleasure. So much pleasure in those lips, those hands.

Later, much later, she untangled herself from him, got out of bed, walked proud, naked to the chair where her bag sat, grabbed a wrapped package out of it.

"Happy Birthday, Alex," she said, handed him his gift.

Alex smiled, took the present, shook it.

"Why do people do that?"

"This?" He shook the package again.

"Yes, that! What if there's something that could break inside?"

"Hmmm... Not here. Feels like a book," he said.

"Okay, I'm off," Sophie said, took a step away from him.

"Nope," grabbed her hand. "Not until I open it."

"You can open it later," she said.

"Nope," pulled her down to sit next to him, on the bed, "I want to open it with you."

Both still naked. Funny how comfortable she was not wearing clothes around him. Sophie had no idea when the awkwardness had disappeared, when it had become so natural between them.

"No card?"

"I-I- just didn't know what to write. I tried. But... oh I don't know," she looked at her hands. He turned to her, lifted her chin with his hand, brushed his lips on hers.

"I know," he said. "Okay, gift."

He ripped the wrapping paper. Two books. The one on top was a coffee table book about beaches and whale watching. Photographs by Zack, words by Hayley, with a beautiful dedication for him. Only for him. He looked at her.

"Thank you." He put it down, spotted the second book. Handmade. His breath faltered.

Chapter Seventy-six

Alex

"The Adventures of the Dread Pirate Alex Alexander and the Incomparable Scarlett Redd – two d's played by her double, Audrey Hepburn." The cover, painted in brilliant, translucent watercolors, depicted a ship mermaid carving, a couple of whales, the dread Pirate Alex, sword in hand, and Scarlett Redd, glorious in red.

A delighted belly laugh escaped his lips. "Wow," he said. "Did you do this?"

"I did."

"Question," he said.

"Answer," she said.

"So, who plays the dread Pirate Alex Alexander if Scarlett Redd is Audrey Hepburn."

"A handsome young man by the name of Alex Carter."

"Then why Audrey Hepburn?"

"Because she's beautiful. Because she's perfect."

You're perfect, he thought.

"I see." He opened the book, went through it page by page. Drawings, photos of their whale watching adventure. Silly words, funny words, touching words.

"Where did you get all these photos?"

"Hayley sent them."

"When?"

"A while ago."

She hadn't shown him. He frowned.

"Why didn't you show them to me?"

She shrugged.

"Why?"

"I'm giving them to you now."

He got to the last page, something happened to his heart. A close up of two faces, facing each other. Sophie, eyes sparkling, smiled up to him. He, enraptured, looked at her face.

"... and, Friends Forever, they sailed the seas for a long long time. The end," she read. "Do you like it?"

"I-I love it," he turned to her, she held his gaze.

"Okay then fifty-four year old. Boy you're old! This wench is leaving you so you can get ready to celebrate your birthday with your daughter. Oh, and this book you can share. Remember, they know all about our whale watching adventure and there's nothing incriminating in it," she dropped a kiss on his cheek, moved to get up.

Nothing incriminating? Just the full force of feelings on his face. He pulled her down, crushed her to his chest, book sandwiched between them, kissed her like his life depended on it.

Chapter Seventy-seven

Sophie

A couple of weeks later, Alex had his arm around Sophie, they walked down the street. It was cold. Rainy. Early dinner with Lu and Olivia. Celebration. Sandra's Boutique needed more jewelry. Sophie's pieces had sold out. Everything was perfect in her life, well almost. Sophie hoped this would be the day Alex showed his daughter he and Sophie were together. Romantically.

"So, better let go of me, Romeo, or they'll suspect I'm your secret lover. The reason your smile is wide, deep and... hard," Sophie teased. She was in a great mood. Three of her four favorite people. Who knew back in Portland she could be so happy?

"Hard is a different part of my anatomy," Alex whispered in her ear, brought her hand to the front of his pants for her to feel.

"Oh you say the sweetest things."

"How about we skip dinner, go back to my place?"

"Nope. They'll know something's up and you don't want anybody to know."

He didn't correct her. They turned the corner.

"I love the rain," Sophie said.

"I know."

"A little dancing in the rain later is in order, wouldn't you say?"

"Depends on where we do the dancing," dropped a kiss on her head.

They reached the main drag in their neighborhood. Her favorite Italian restaurant was hopping tonight. Lu and Olivia, already seated by the window, toasted. Alex dropped his arm from Sophie's shoulders, put a little distance between them. She felt the coldness seep into her side, into her heart. They'd been doing this dance exactly three months, nine days, since that first night. Almost every night since she got back from Florida. She couldn't get enough of him. Everything seemed perfect, except...

Lu spotted them, waved. Alex opened the door for Sophie. She entered. The hot, sweet air perfumed with garlic, spices, wine, hit her nose. She took a deep breath. She loved Italian food.

"So what'll be today, sweet Sophie?" Alex whispered in her ear. Sweet? She hadn't felt sweet with what she'd done to his body last night. Savage more like it.

"Mmmm I could think of one thing I'd like to eat right about now," she said, most innocent expression reflected on her face. They'd stopped at the entrance for a moment. She felt him tense, put a little more distance between them. "Oh, you meant food," she laughed. "So many choices. So many."

"Sophie..." he said, nervous.

"Okay, okay. Back to food. Maybe pasta Bolognese. No, chicken Piccatta. Cheesecake. Oh, I don't know."

"How about we order different things and share?"

"See that's what makes it impossible for me to hate you."

"Hate me? Is that even an option?"

"Hate is always an option, young man."

"I hate it when you call me young man."

"See?"

"I don't like it, Sophie."

"Why? You're younger than me therefore you're a young man."

"It puts distance between us."

"Kinda like the distance you put between us then."

He tensed. She'd got to him. She knew. She just couldn't help herself. Sophie understood it was his decision, his choice, to tell his daughter. To let everybody see this thing between them. It was one of the rules. Still...

"But right now I adore you because you're gonna share food with me!" She nodded at Lu they were coming.

"Hey! You're late," Olivia said.

"You're early. We're right on time," Alex kissed his daughter's cheek.

"You ordered appetizers," Sophie beamed.

"And your favorite Prosecco," Lu handed Sophie a flute filled with the pink bubbly liquid.

"I'm having a martini," Alex said, headed to the bar.

"Make that two," Lu said.

"Three olives," Alex stated.

Lu nodded.

"So..." Olivia said to Sophie.

"What?"

Lu looked at Olivia.

"What are you two up to?" Sophie asked.

"A little nosh. A little bubbly," Lu said.

Alex got back to the table, took the seat between Olivia and Sophie.

"Now," Lu mouthed to Olivia.

"So Alex... what's up with you two?" Olivia asked.

"What? Up? What do you mean?"

Sophie looked at Lu. Lu shrugged.

"You and Sophie?"

"Sophie - what? Nothing. Why?"

Sophie felt his panic rise, leaned back. She'd let him take this one. All on his own. He was the one with the problem. He'd be the one to answer.

"You're always together. Tied at the hip."

"Honey, we live next door to each other."

"What's with the looks, Alex?" Olivia continued.

"Would it kill you to call me Dad every once in a while?"

"Okay, Dad, what's with not taking your eyes off Sophie? What's with all the touching? Anything you want to tell me?"

Sophie turned to Lu. Lu smiled. Sophie shook her head.

"I don't know what you're talking about. Sophie and I are just friends. That's all. Nothing more. Ever. Friends. You know that."

"Hmmm..." Lu said, reached under the table, squeezed Sophie's hand. Sophie shifted her gaze to Lu, smile frozen on her lovely face.

"You and I are just friends, right Sophie? You know me," his voice high, trapped.

"'Cause I'd be okay if you, you know..." Olivia said.

"What?" Alex asked, "What Olivia?"

"If you were together together, you know."

"Honey, you know I'm a one woman man," Alex avoided Sophie's face. "Always. I fool around sometimes, but it's not real, you know that, honey. It's always been your mother. No room for anyone else." A punch to Sophie's gut. "My heart belongs to your mother." Alex gulped. "And what would Sophie want with an idiot like me, huh? She's too beautiful for me. Too wonderful for me. I'm not good enough for her. Right, Sophe?" His eyes pleaded.

And there it was. A second punch. Sophie's heart cracked, hardened. No future. Just sex. Secret sex. It'd been shocking in the beginning, scary, then fun, but somewhere along the way things changed. For her. She wanted more. Needed more. Lu found Sophie's hand again, tightened around it.

"Right," Sophie said. "Why would I want an old man like your dad when a younger man could enjoy all of this deliciousness." Hard, avoided Alex's desperate look.

When a man tells his truth, believe him. Words Annie uttered after Sophie's heart had been broken for the third time when they were in college. Men always mean what they say and Alex, after all, was a man. And he'd spoken his truth many times. She knew his truth by heart, but only now had her heart heard it. It finally registered.

Alex looked at Sophie, tentative, "Oh, so now I'm an old man?"

Sophie looked straight in Alex's eyes, hoping. All she saw were nerves, fear, a kind of pleading, asking her to say nothing. To admit to nothing. To deny everything. To avoid everything. To let him off the hook. A mountain of bricks flattened her heart, hardened her heart. Eyes open, she got it. He had given all he was capable of giving. But was that enough for her? Would she be happy with the crumbs he threw her way? No matter their connection, the mind-blowing sex, the chemistry, the way he looked at her when they were in bed, the look that told her exactly how he felt about her. He would never admit it to himself. To her. He was so comfortable in his misery, in his self-pity, in his love for Mattie that there was no room for Sophie in his heart, in his life. In his bed, yes. In the afternoons, just the two of them, watching the sunset, yes. There yes. In the outside world, where he would have to admit he could feel love once again, no. There, a hard no. No room for Sophie, older, silly woman who made him laugh, who made him feel, who made him love. Love... her heart knew he loved her but... Hit her right now, right here. It was never going to happen. He'd told her. She'd just forgotten. She thought he would change, but she knew better. Men don't change. They are who they are. They tell you. Believe them when they do. Believe them. She did. Now.

"Sophe," Alex said, soft. "Hey, where did you go?"

Back to reality. Eyes a little bright, she painted on a smile.

"Sorry, went away for a moment," Sophie avoided his eyes.

"You okay?" Alex said.

"Always. Hey, just had a thought. Anyone for doing something crazy?" Sophie asked.

"Of course, darling," Lu said.

"Depends," Alex said, scared.

"I'm kinda feeling like getting a second tattoo."

"Yes!" Olivia said. "I'm in!"

"Settled then. Big Ben, here we come."

"I don't think that's a good idea, Sophie."

"Oh Alex, it is such a good idea. Time I heeded your advice and got myself a lover, don't you think?"

No, no. Rules. No. Not Benjamin, no, Alex thought. "No," Alex said.

"Why not?" Sophie asked.

"Because he's gorgeous, hung like a horse, young, and asks about Sophie every time I see him," Lu said, sweet.

"That's true," Olivia said. "He keeps coming to yoga hoping to run into you, Sophe, he likes you."

Sophie spotted the alarm in his eyes.

"No, not him," Alex said.

"Why?" Sophie looked directly at Alex.

"I just think you need someone different, is all."

"Like who?" Sophie said.

"Oh, I don't know."

"Well, when you do know, please let me know." Sophie downed the flute of Prosecco in one gulp. Lu filled her glass again.

Chapter Seventy-eight

Sophie

"What was that about, Sophe?" Alex asked. Walking home, his arm around her shoulder. "You didn't back me up."

Sophie inched a little away from him.

"I thought we agreed. This is between you and me."

"I didn't say anything."

"But Olivia knew. She asked."

"Knew what, Alex? That we're sleeping together? I don't think so."

"But she asked."

"She asked if there was something between us, because it's evident."

"I-I've been so careful."

"Yes," she shrugged.

"We're friends, aren't we?" Pulled her closer.

Friends. Yes. They were friends. Friends with benefits. Friends who shared everything except what Sophie wanted most. Friends who did not share love, well one of them didn't. One of them did. Every day she showed Alex how much she loved him. A smile, a touch, her body, her everything. Alex barely noticed. Or forced himself to be blind, to not see. Yes, he spent all his free time with her. Could not keep his hands off her, his mouth, his body. Touched her whenever she was near, whenever they were alone. Alone. Made love to her, no, not that. Fucked her. Sophie needed to remember. That's all it was. Fucking. Not lovemaking, except it felt that way every night. Every night she gave. Granted, she had not let him completely in, but the protective crust around her heart had a small crack. He'd snuck in. She'd let him in. So, he wanted just a friendship. Then that's what it'll be. Last time, Sophie thought. This would be the last time she'd share her body with him. Better save their precious friendship. Time to say good-bye, time to patch the crack, push him out. Time to hide. Time to run.

Sophie took another step away from Alex, his arm fell off her shoulder. His hand reached out, threaded his fingers with hers. "Sophe," he said, searched her eyes. "You're not really getting a tattoo, right?"

She looked at her feet.

"Rule number two?" he whispered.

Rules were meant to be broken, Sophie thought. After all, she'd broken the golden rule. She'd fallen for him.

"Sophie?"

"Oh, Alex, maybe. Why not?"

"Because..."

"Why, Alex, give me one good reason, aside from the rules, why I should not get a tattoo."

"Benjamin."

"I'd say Benjamin is exactly the reason why I should."

Alex stopped, let go of her hand, turned to her.

"Sophie," he said, eyes filled with hurt. He grabbed her face, leaned in for a kiss.

"Stop it, young man," she whispered. "We're outside and you don't want anyone to see us, remember?"

Chapter Seventy-nine

Alex

Sophie moaned. Alex nuzzled her neck, her spot, the one which gave her goosebumps, the one that melted her, made her want more of him. All of him. She giggled, he closed the gap, forced his lips to hers. He knew where to touch her, how to touch her. How to love her. God, she was delicious. He was inside of her, her sex cocooning his, pumping into her like there was no tomorrow. He felt her urgency, matched her stroke for stroke. What had gotten into her? After the talk of Benjamin had died down, she'd been unusually quiet. He'd seen the wheels turning in her head at dinner, like she was trying to make a decision. Something had changed but right now he didn't care. All that mattered was Sophie, in his bed. Loving him. Loving him? No. No. Not that. She whispered his name, almost at her point. He moved faster, deeper, harder.

Later, Sophie stirred, untwined her body from his. He felt her withdrawal.

"Sophe," he whispered.

"Hmm."

"What's up?"

She closed her eyes. He sensed distance.

"What's up," he asked again.

"What do you mean?" She broke the final thread of their physical connection, raised her elbow, placed her head on her hand. Looked directly into his eyes.

"You. This."

"I don't know what you mean."

"Sophie, we're good together. You know we are. I'm happy with you. You are so damned sexy I can't get enough of you. Your skin. Your scent. Your -"

"My body, I know, Alex. I know."

"Sophie, please."

"What do you want from me? The rules are set in stone with you. I'm here. Right now. Today."

He said nothing. He had nothing to say.

"You know this is going to end, right?"

That shook him. "No, I mean, what do you mean?"

"You and me. Here and only here."

"Does it have to?" Alex asked.

"You tell me."

Again he was quiet.

"You don't want Olivia to know. It's been three months, this secret of ours."

"Three months, nine days," he whispered.

"Okay. You know how many days, yet you don't want anybody to know. I think you don't even want you to know. Why is that, you think?"

Alex knew the answer. He knew he wasn't ready to make it real. It was never going to be real. He wanted her. That was real. All of her, even her heart, but he couldn't give her his. Not totally. It belonged to Mattie. Olivia would not understand if he were serious about another woman. Except he wanted this woman, Sophie, all the time. But just the two of them. In their little cocoon where he didn't have to admit to the world, to his world, that he'd fallen. For her. His Sophie. She invaded his thoughts all the time. She'd inched her way into the crack that split his heart in two, putting it back together, slow, steady. But he wasn't ready. He never would be. He'd made a vow.

"Alex, I get you can't, you won't. So don't ask me to. My friendship is what you want, that you've got."

"Sophie, you know..." he trailed off.

"I know."

"I-I can't"

"I know," her eyes filled.

He looked at her beautiful face illuminated by the moonlight coming from the bedroom window. Smiled. Remembered how many times Sophie made him dance in the moonlight. How much fun he had with her. With her. Always with her. Her face broke him, always. He reached out, ran the back of his hand down her cheek. A tear rolled down her face, onto the back of his hand. She leaned into the caress, closed her eyes, leaned forward, grazed his lips with hers. Deepened the kiss, quiet, desperate. Final.

"What's up, Sophe?" He asked, soft.

"Gotta go," she said after a long moment of silence. Her eyes on his. Alex panicked a little. She never left his bed. Always stayed 'til morning. He was the one who left her bed, stole out at the last possible moment, when his heart started to feel. Before his heart started to feel.

Sophie moved away from him. He grabbed her hand, pulled it to his lips. "Stay."

"No," barely a whisper.

"You always stay."

"Not today."

"Why?"

"I want to go," she said, sad. Alex tried to stop her from getting up. She slipped off. "Sweet dreams, young man."

Young man. She wanted distance between them. He hated it. He shook his head, an iron hand settled on his heart. He jumped out of bed, gathered her in his arms. Her softness made him hard. He wanted her, could not let go. Wanted her again. And again. He was greedy.

Wanted all of her, unable to give the same. Sophie kissed him, he tasted salt on his lips.

"Good bye, young man."

Chapter Eighty

Sophie

Sophie closed the door of her cottage, leaned her back on it, slid down to the floor. Her shirt inside out, panties, bra in hand. She heard Alex's footsteps climb the stairs. Why was she so upset? The deal had been made between them. No love. Just fun. Sex. Companionship. But she wanted more, damn it. More. She wanted it all. And Mattie's memory hung between them. Another picture of her added to the dresser. Small, but there. His screen saver, Mattie. His love, Mattie. Always Mattie. Everything Mattie. A reminder of what she had with Alex could never be. He'd never love her. Didn't want to love her. Not her. Never. She'd noticed it weeks ago, didn't compute until today. Today, at dinner, it finally hit home. All of it. No doubts. Not anymore.

No hope.

"Sophie," Alex whispered, knocked two times on the wood.

Sophie raised her hand, clicked the lock, heard Alex take a breath.

"Don't lock me out. Please."

"Go home, Alex."

"What did I do?"

"I'm tired," tears streamed down her face, her voice barely a whisper.

"Please, Sophie. Can we talk?"

"Tomorrow."

"I need you."

Such a man. Always about him. He needed her. He wanted her. What about what she needed, wanted? Sophie had given him everything. Well, almost everything. She'd let him crack the protection around her heart, she'd let him creep in, but just like she'd let him in, she'd push him out. She didn't want to be the ridiculous older woman crazy in love with a younger, unavailable man. Shit! She was in love. Crazy in love with him. Sophie closed her eyes, thought about a French movie she'd seen when she was in her twenties. She'd been obsessed with it then, watched it over and over again. Gorgeous, thin, successful, perfect French woman tangled in a sexual affair with a beautiful, sexy young man. Man, he was beautiful. The woman had been maybe forty-five, he in his late twenties. Steamy sex, intense. For her. For him just taking a woman he fancied. Something to do. Sophie thought back then she never wanted anyone to hurt her like that, to discard her when he'd had enough. And now, she was that woman. She had to stop herself from feeling, from wanting. The end of the movie popped in her head. The lovers apart, she devastated, he moved on with his life, not a though to her pain. The woman went to Greece, jumped into the ocean, cleansed herself of his touch. A desperate song set the scene for the end. Sophie had fallen in love with that song. Listened to it whenever her heart had been broken. Time to break the connection. Time to listen to the song. Time to walk away.

Sophie heard Alex's body inch down to the ground on the other side of the door.

"Sophie."

She froze. How did he know she was still there?

"I can feel you. Open the door, please."

Mind reader. She said nothing.

"What did I do? What can I do for you to let me in?"

You can let me in, you asshole, she thought. *You can give me space in that heart of yours that I want, need. You can tell me you love me, not only that you want me, that you need me, that you can't get enough of me but that you love me. You can stop being so damned gorgeous. I want you to make love to me, you jerk, not to fuck me. Love me. Me*, she thought. *You can love me.*

Except it was never going to happen. He'd told her. She knew his heart belonged to Mattie, only Mattie. And if she had learned something, anything, about men in her almost sixty years, is men always tell the truth. When they tell you they're not good enough for you, believe them. When they tell you work is more important than you, believe them. When they tell you they will only love one person, even if that person is dead, believe them. *Believe him, Sophie. Believe him. Alex will never love you like you ache to be loved. Sure he can play with you. For a while. If you get in any deeper there will be no recovery. Not for you. Better to cut your losses now. Better to let him go. Now.*

Sophie took a breath, visualized the crack in her heart where he'd snuck in start to close, another layer of crust protecting her from his embarrassment of their relationship. That's what she'd seen today at dinner. An affair, yes, let's do it but letting his daughter know about them, well that had been a hard no. Lu knew, kept her secret. Sophie suspected Olivia knew as well, but said nothing. Until tonight when she asked the question.

Alex told her when they first met he would not love again. She believed him. Now.

"What did I do?"

"Nothing, Alex. You did nothing. It's me. All me. Just go home."

"What can I do?"

"If you have to ask," barely a whisper.

Chapter Eighty-one

Alex

Alex felt Sophie move away from the door, not a word to him. She walked away. Left him cold, sad. Alone. He knew this was a crucial moment. He knew what she needed. To know she was important to him. Not as a friend but as so much more. To be out in the open. She probably thought he was ashamed of their affair. That was not it. If he let it happen he'd be admitting to the world he loved her. That he could not do. He could not give her love. His body, yes. His heart, well it was another matter entirely. Scared the shit out of him to love again. What if he lost her? What if she left him like Mattie had? What if she died? A breath caught in his throat. No survival a second time. No.

He stayed by the door a long time. Imagined her in bed now, her bed, not his. Already asleep. Maybe if he stayed glued to her door the connection between them would not break.

Something had changed tonight. What had he done? He'd been straight with her from the beginning. Why couldn't things stay the same? Friends during the day. Sunsets together. Her hand in his. His body craving hers, then Sophie wrapped around him in bed. Once, twice, three times. Forever. She'd wake up in his arms at his place. He'd steal away before dawn at hers. Tonight had been different. She'd been the one who walked away.

He'd waited for her to come out of her cottage for her usual morning walk. Waited ten minutes, fifteen. Nothing. He'd walked to her door, looked in the window. Everything was still. Quiet. Was she still asleep? He knocked, soft, then harder, desperate. Silence. Again.

"Sophie?"

He moved around the perimeter of the cottage. Her car? Gone. Where had she gone so early? Damn. She was going to be hard to pin down today. Hard to convince not to dump him. If only she hadn't locked him out last night. If only she'd let him hold her again, kiss her again Love her again. If only she'd talked to him he would have erased the pain with kisses, cracked the crust around her heart with his body, his... love?

He could not say the word, feel the word, live the word. Impossible. He could not let go of his past. Let go?

No, Sophie, no. He'd be damned if he'd let go of Sophie. No letting Sophie go. Not today. Not ever.

Alex reached for his phone, dialed Sophie. Straight to voicemail. Her cottage dark. Her car gone. Lu! Of course she'd gone to Lu. Wait! Benjamin? No, God, please not Benjamin. Not Benjamin. Alex turned, giant leaps to his garage, jumped in his truck, backed out the driveway, screeched down the road.

Chapter Eighty-two

Sophie

Lu handed Sophie a flute of Prosecco. "It's six-thirty in the morning, Lu."

"Not in Italy it's not. Drink."

Lu, stunning in a blue negligee, matched the color of her eyes with the ocean in Positano. Sophie knew this because Lu told her.

"The man is an idiot," Lu said.

Sophie's nose red, eyes puffy. "I don't know why I can't stop crying. He didn't do anything. Everything's as it always was."

"Precisely, but not in your heart. You let him in. You're in love with him."

"I don't want to be."

"But you are."

"What do I do now? I can't face him. It hurts too much. He told me how it was with him the moment we met. I know he can't give me more. I want more. I feel ridiculous wanting him. I want him so much, Lu. So much."

"You have him."

"You know I don't."

"You do. He just doesn't know it. Yet."

"His body, yes."

"Be brave, *libelula*, say it."

"I can't."

"*Fifona* then."

Sophie snorted a laugh.

"God, how I wish I'd sat on Benjamin's lap. My heart was safe with Big Ben. And I never got to experience the experience of the man."

"Well, darling, that can certainly be arranged. Did you not say your left boob needed a little ink? I'm sure the boy would be happy to comply. Only if you promise to go through with it. Trust me. Worth every stroke."

"Don't be gross."

"Gross? It was divine, *fifona*, divine! Almost a religious experience."

"You do him then."

"I've done him."

God, Lu could make her laugh. Always. She wanted to be just like her. So free. So comfortable with her body, with her... 'womaness'. With her curves. Confident enough to admit to a man that she loved him.

That she wanted all of him and would not be content with just a few crumbs.

"All or nothing, *libelula*."

Sophie's eyes filled.

"Not the waterworks again," Lu topped off her glass. "Not England then?"

Sophie shook her head no.

"Italy then. We go to Italy."

Chapter Eighty-three

Alex

Where the hell was Sophie? He'd kept an ear out for the sound of her car, the feel of her, the scent of her. Anything Sophie. Where was she? It was almost time for their afternoon ritual. He'd driven by Benjamin's, scared shitless to find her car there. He'd breathed relief. Not there. Lu's gate had been firmly closed, he'd peeked but no sign of Sophie's Volvo there. Somehow he knew she was there. Or had she gone to Portland? Annie was not in Portland, she was in Florida. Had Sophie escaped to Florida? Again? He pulled out his cell, searched for a voicemail, a text. Nothing. He'd called. Voicemail. He'd left messages. Five to be exact, two hang-ups. Twenty texts. No response. He wanted to talk, to erase the pain he knew he'd caused. What the hell was wrong with him? Why couldn't he give her what she wanted? What she hadn't asked for but he knew she needed? He knew she was uncomfortable with their age difference. The almost seven years, made her feel inadequate, not good enough. Him keeping their relationship secret proved her insecurity right. She was not important for him to risk everything for her. Not important to be a partner, a real partner in his life. Not important for him to love.

But she was. Important. Very. She was everything. The last face he saw when he laid his head to sleep, the first thought when he woke. Sophie's smile. Sophie's eyes. Sophie's laugh. Sophie's body. Sophie, always Sophie since the day she showed up at his door, asked if he was the neighborhood handyman. It'd been a very long time since anyone was everything to him. It'd been eleven years... what? He'd stopped counting the days. When? When had he stopped counting? Could it be?

"Sophie, where are you, damn it?" Alex whispered.

The sound of her car. He sprinted out the door, spotted Sophie's car rounding the driveway.

"Sophie," he rushed out. The car stopped. He yanked the driver's door open.

"Olivia!"

"Alex, what the hell!"

"Where's Sophie? Why are you driving Sophie's car? Is she okay?"

"Yeah, she's fine."

"Where is she?" Edge in his voice.

"What do you care?"

"Well, she's my neighbor."

"Let's go with that then."

"I was worried. She's been gone all day."

"Not the first time she's gone all day, Alex."

"Is she okay? Just want to make sure she's okay."

"Ah, okay, Dad, if that's it, she's fine. You have nothing to worry about."

"I-is she with Benjamin? Is she getting a tattoo?" Jaw clenched.

"Not right now, no."

Alex closed his eyes, ran a hand through his hair.

Chapter Eighty-four

Sophie

Lu had confiscated Sophie's cell. No to temptation.

"Let him stew, darling. No communication. Let him really experience what life is like without Sophie."

Ian Brenner, tall, lean, silvered hair fox, waited outside the Naples Airport. Lu spotted him, straightened her back, smiled.

"Wow, you weren't kidding, Lu. He's gorgeous," Sophie said, sunglasses covered her puffy, swollen eyes. Halfway across the Atlantic she'd fallen asleep, stopped crying.

"So?" Sophie asked when she noticed Lu's reaction to the handsome man.

"What?"

"Husband number four?"

Chapter Eighty-five

Sophie

Heaven, thought Sophie. Or it would be if she weren't so sad. Devastated, more likely. She missed him. With every pore in her body she missed Alex. But she needed to run. To think. To decide what to do next. Away from him. Should she let him in, take whatever bit of himself he was willing to give? Maybe. Should she let him go? Move on? Let the crust that covered her heart thicken, close the gap through which he slipped in? Too late. He was in already. Firm. Planted. Alex's heart, body, inside. He was in.

"Not going to give you back your phone," Lu said, the car Ian drove presented the sparkling water below, the color of Lu's eyes. She hadn't lied. The mountains speckled with towns, trees, color. A breath caught in Sophie's throat. She took in the magnificence of the landscape before her. God, this Earth was beautiful. Took her breath away. Respect. Awe. Wonder.

"What?" Sophie asked, her eyes never left the window, the narrow road edged to the precipice. Fitting metaphor for this point in her life. She could continue down the winding road, towards a new future. Fall into the precipice of life without Alex, without love but into the sparkling waves of the Adriatic. Or she could go back. She could always go back and accept whatever Alex was willing to offer. However little, it was more than she ever thought she'd have, she deserved. *Go back...* said her heart.

"Distance, Sophe."

"I know, Lu." She did know. Really know. "I'm the one who needs distance, remember? That's why we're here. So I can think. Decide." And stop feeling.

Chapter Eighty-six

Alex

Sweaty, startled, empty, angry, sad. Alex groaned, turned, untangled his long, muscular legs from the sheets that kept him prisoner. Scratched his chin, week-old stubble itched like crazy. Sleep eluded him for days. When he did sleep, Sophie's face haunted him, whispered in his ear to love her. What was he going to do? He'd called every day for the last two weeks, five days, seventeen hours. Yes, he kept count of the days without Sophie. His Sophie. He'd called her more times than he could count. Sometimes just dialed her number to hear her voice on the other side of her voicemail message. Sometimes pleading words, begged for her to answer the next time, to return his call. Anything, not this frightening silence that sliced him in half. Olivia refused to tell him anything. He knew she knew where Sophie was. Lu answered his call once, told him to leave Sophie alone. That was the one thing he could not do, would not do. No.

A ding had him reaching for his phone, hope in his heart. A smile filled his face. Sophie. She'd texted. Thank God. She'd asked him for time. Time was the one thing he'd already given her. Two weeks, five days, seventeen hours.

Alex: Sophie, please, I need to hear your voice. Come back. Please. Call me. Please.

He'd begged. Waited. Waited. "Please," he'd whispered. Please.

Silence.

Chapter Eighty-seven

Sophie

Campari Orange, the most delicious drink Sophie had discovered sitting on a terrace café that overlooked the water, under a lemon tree. The color of sunset. The scent of citrus mingled with sea air. But no, she was not going to think of that sunset. This sunset. Italy. Only sunset on her mind right now was the one before her. Liar.

The bitter red of the liquor intermingled with the sweetness of the perfect Italian orange exploded in deliciousness inside her mouth. Heaven. Another metaphor for her life, bittersweet. Delicious heartbreak.

She and Lu had shopped all afternoon. Shoes, Italian shoes everywhere. She'd bought three pairs. A dinner dress because, who knows what dinners she'd have in the very near future. Ian promised many. Gave her hope. She wasn't ready to go back home. Nope. The wound still fresh. No peace yet for her. And Italy was so...

wonderful. If she had to rebuild her heart once again, this was the place.

"Luciana, *ciao*," a handsome, elegant man kissed Lu's cheek.

"Franco," Lu got up, hugged him.

Wow, Sophie thought, *Italians are incredibly good-looking.* Franco looked at Sophie, eyes twinkled, smile wide, inviting.

"Franco, this is Sophie Alexander. Sophie, Franco Amaro," Lu said.

"*Piacere*," Franco kissed Sophie's hand, Sophie giggled.

"Join us for a drink," Lu said.

Franco took a seat next to Lu, turned to Sophie, "So Miss Alexander, you like our little part of the world?"

"Love it. I want to stay here forever," Sophie said, knew it was a lie but it felt true at this particular moment. Here she was safe. Here she would forget. Here she would heal.

Later that night, Lu, Ian and Sophie finished dinner on the terrace at Lu's apartment.

"Franco fell in love with Sophie today," Lu said.

Ian laughed. "Franco falls in love every day."

"I liked him. Sweet," Sophie said.

"Smooth," Lu said. "He wants you, Sophe, I know him."

Would it be so bad to have a fling with Franco? Could she do it? Would it erase the need for Alex's hands, mouth, body... heart? Maybe. Maybe not.

Chapter Eighty-eight

Alex

"You look like hell, man," Liam said.

"Thank you, Sunshine," Alex said. "Whiskey, double."

Liam grabbed the glass, filled it with liquid, placed it in front of Alex. It was early enough so the Pub was quiet.

"She left you, huh?"

Alex looked up at Liam.

"Ah, c'mon, you're really not that stupid to think I didn't know."

"Know?"

"Sophie, man."

"What are you talking about? What about Sophie?"

"I've known you're crazy about her since she moved to town."

"What?"

"Everybody knows. You're the only idiot who doesn't."

"It's not really like that. We're friends."

"Uh-huh. Yes, friends who do more than friendship. Alex, wake-up, man. What are you waiting for? I get it with all the other women, but this one... she's special. She fits with you. She brought you back to life, dude."

"We're friends, Liam. Friends," he downed the liquid in one gulp.

"Okay. So you don't care that she left town then?"

"I care."

"But just as a friend, right? You don't really care when she comes back, right? Or who she comes back with, right?"

"What do you mean who she comes back with?"

"Things happen when you're on vacation. Women meet men. Hook up. Fall in love."

What the fuck?

"Do you know where she is?" Alex growled.

"No man, I just know who she went with. Lu, you know, the queen of love, the queen of fun."

Fuck!

Chapter Eighty-nine

Sophie

Italian food markets. Heaven. Fresh tomatoes exploded flavor in your mouth, green leafy arugula added a bitter taste to counteract the sweetness. Fresh pasta, fresh figs, fresh fish, fresh peaches, lemons, all sizes, many shapes. And gelato. Oh, the orgasmic flavor of the Italian gelato. *Nocciola, Stracciatella, Bacio, Nutella, Fragola, Limone,* Sophie sampled them all. She'd been in need of extra boyfriend comfort since she left the US. An Italian *fidanzato,* i.e. fiancé because she'd decided she'd marry Italian. The creaminess of the gelato eased the pain in her heart, at least for the time it melted in her mouth. Because pain she had, and pain would stay with her. How to get over Alex? How? God, she wished she'd never... Never what? Never fallen into his bed. She could have kept her feelings in check, her heart guarded, imprisoned in the dark protective crust. But having kissed him, loved him, it was going to be impossible to get over him. She'd have to find a cliff, a small one, because after all she was a *fifona*, to jump into the cleansing waters of the sparkling Adriatic Sea. Rid the memory of his hands on her right off her body. Wash her love free.

Sophie's phone buzzed. A text. She looked. Not Alex. Relief. Disappointment.

Lu: Darling, can you pick up an extra pint of ice cream? Wink emoji. Franco's coming to dinner.

Franco, Sophie thought. Handsome. Sexy. Smart. Flirt. Why the hell not?

Sophie: Sure thing.

Why could it not be Alex at dinner? Alex. Damn him. Sophie ached to talk to him, to hear his voice, to read his texts and she had. Listened, read. Over and over and over again since Lu had given her phone back. Her heart ready to dial his number, hear him out. Her head prevented her from calling, forgiving, begging him to come get her. She'd texted once exactly four days ago. 'I need time to sort myself out.' His response immediate, pleading with her to come back, but he never said the magic words. Not once in all the texts, in all the messages. Not once. She understood what she wanted was impossible. Time to cut her losses. What better place to erase the feel of his skin, his mouth, his presence than in the breathtaking Amalfi Coast?

Sophie shook all thoughts of Alex away from her mind, concentrated on a beautiful Branzino for the feast she planned for that evening. Dinner al fresco, under the lemon trees, overlooking the Adriatic, with Lu and Ian. And now Franco, too. Franco, gorgeous Italian heartbreaker. Tonight, she might even flirt back. And why not? Good for the soul.

Sophie's phone buzzed. A phone call. Olivia. She'd missed her young friend.

"Hey, Olivia," Sophie answered, big smile.

"Sophie." It wasn't Olivia. "It's me," Alex said.

"Oh."

"Please, please, don't hang up. Please. Give me a chance. I miss you. So much," his voice trembled.

"I need time."

"You've had three weeks and four days," Alex said.

"You're counting?" She whispered.

"Sophie."

"I need more time."

"How much more time?"

"I don't know."

"Are you still mad at me?"

"I was never mad at you."

"But you left. And you don't want to talk to me."

"To think. To process. Away from you."

"Sophie, please."

"Alex," stepped away from the fishmonger, rubbed the space between her eyebrows, found a spot that overlooked the water. "Okay, maybe we do need to talk. Maybe it's time."

"Where are you?"

Ignored his question. "Look, this is all on me. You told me the truth from the beginning. You were very clear. It's all me. I-I... fell in love with you, Alex. I know that wasn't part of our deal. But it happened and I'm sorry."

"You're sorry you fell in love with me?"

"No. I'm sorry I broke our deal."

"Sophie, Sophie, come back. This is a conversation we need to have face to face."

He hadn't said he loved her. Not even a little. She'd been fearless, she'd left her beloved *fifona* behind. Spoken her truth. Told him she loved him. But he... he didn't love her.

"This is better for me. Easier to say what I need to say if you're not in front of me," Sophie said. *If I don't have your beautiful face that I want to kiss, your hands I long to hold, your chest...* Sophie thought.

"Where are you, Sophie?"

"Shopping for fish."

She heard Alex laugh on the other side of the phone.

"What time is it where you are?" he asked.

"Like I'm going to tell you, young man."

"I hate it-"

"I know," she interrupted. "But the fact is you are younger than me." And she needed distance. Lots of it. As if an ocean were not enough.

"I don't care."

"I do."

"Okay, but this is something we can do nothing about. Seven years, big deal."

"Almost eight."

"I don't care."

"There is also the fact that you don't want to be in a relationship with anyone."

"We are in a relationship."

"I mean in a real relationship with someone who is alive." She heard him take in a breath, knew she'd poked his wound, she continued, "I don't say this to hurt you, Alex, to be mean, just stating a fact. You were very clear with me on my porch, remember, when we first met, before there was anything between us. You were open and honest with me. Rules. One of them, for me, is when a man speaks his truth, I listen, I believe. My marriage ended because I didn't believe him. He told me who he was. I thought I could change him. Men don't change because we want them to change. It is as it should be."

"I can change."

"I don't want you to. You're perfect. A beautiful, perfect, wounded man."

"Sophie, please."

"This is all me, Alex. This is what I do. You know that, I told you. I close my heart and that is exactly what I need to do now. I need to be away from you so I can get over loving you."

"I don't want you to get over me, Sophie. I want you to come back. I need you. I want you so much. I want ice cream with you, sunsets with you. I want you. All the time."

Still not a magic word in sight.

"I'll be back when we can be friends. New rules. New friends, okay?" Sophie said.

"Please, Sophie."

"I gotta go. Cooking dinner for Lu, Ian and Franco tonight. Just spotted a beautiful heirloom tomato with my name on it. Good-bye, Alex," she disconnected the phone, turned it off.

"And a gallon or two of gelato."

Except she didn't want ice cream today.

Chapter Ninety

Alex

"Who the hell is Franco?" They were in his kitchen. Olivia gave him the stink eye. He'd taken her phone without her permission, dialed Sophie. He knew Sophie would answer Olivia's call. He needed her, her voice, her closeness, even if only in his ear.

"What do you care?" Olivia snatched her phone back.

"I care! Who is he? Is he sleeping with Sophie?" His head filled with images of Sophie naked in someone else's arms, of her pleasure, her eyes closed, her mouth moaning someone else's name. Not his. Franco's.

"Maybe."

"Olivia."

"Why Dad, why do you want to know?"

"I have to."

"It really is none of your business who Sophie sleeps with. Is there a reason why it should matter to you?"

"Olivia, please. Tell me."

"No Dad, let her be."

"I can't."

"Why? Why can't you?"

Alex closed his eyes, felt his heart break in two.

"Because I'm in love with her," he whispered. "I love her. And because if she does not..." He could not finish the sentence. No. That was not going to happen. Sophie loved him. She did. Almost as much as he loved her. Almost.

"Stupid, stupid man. Took you long enough to say it."

Chapter Ninety-one

Sophie

"I believe someone has a birthday today," a soft breeze brought a whisper to Sophie's ear. Sunset. Lu's terrace on the Amalfi Coast provided a show like few offer. Soft pillows on her back, Sophie sat under a lemon tree brimming with fruit. The scent of the leaves surrounded her, shielded her, eased her heartache. Sophie closed her eyes for one second, let herself feel the loss wash over her. Yes. Today was her sixtieth birthday. Milestone. Sexy, sensational, sixty, she'd joked that morning at breakfast with Lu and Ian. They offered to take her out for dinner. Sophie wanted to be alone.

"Rain check? Tomorrow?" Sophie asked.

"You sure?" Lu said.

Funny, Lu hadn't insisted, decided to stay the night at Ian's place, give her some space.

"I am. Need a little time to switch gears, you know, to stop all this," she touched her heart.

"So stop hiding all the pain. Let it rip."

"My ritual is happening. Tonight."

"Dancing in the moonlight?"

"Always," Sophie said a little sad. Okay, a lot.

Sixty. Hmmm. Nothing different. The pain that ripped her heart in two still there. Dull, sharp, penetrating.

She'd planned a little ritual. Bought a couple of candles, a bouquet of pink and yellow roses, a pint of *Nutella* gelato, chosen boyfriend for the occasion. And she planned to dance. Maybe even jump in the water. Let it all go. Try for a new beginning.

"Sophie..." a whisper in her ear, a voice she imagined everyday. God, she was pathetic. Is this what happens when one turns sixty? Senility? She shook her head, laughed out loud, took a swig of the Prosecco, her third today. Her Birthday, just another day. Without Alex.

"You sharing the boyfriend today?" the voice closer, she felt the brush of lips on the back of her neck. What the hell?

"Alex?" Sophie closed her eyes again, hoped to erase the feeling of Alex. She'd imagined his voice, his breath on her skin, the way her body responded to his.

"Sophie," Alex moved, took the seat next to hers on the love seat. Her eyes flew open, she turned, looked into a pair of dark eyes.

Chapter Ninety-two

Alex.

"You keep running away," Alex said, heart beat wild, anxious... hopeful.
"It's what I do."
"The dragonfly should have been a chicken."
"Yeah," she said.
"I stay," he said, reached for her hand. Sophie tried to move it away, but he threaded his fingers through hers, pulled it to his mouth, grazed his lips over her knuckles. "I stay when it's real."
Sophie turned her gaze to the ocean before them.
"This is real, Sophie."
"Is it?" barely a whisper.
He nodded. "I told Olivia," he whispered, eyes searched her profile. She kept her gaze firmly on the horizon. "She already knew."
"I didn't tell her," she said.
"You didn't need to."

"I told Lu. From the beginning. Lu knew. And Annie. Made Lu swear not to tell Olivia."

"She didn't."

"Then how?"

"Sophie, Sophie, I tried so hard not to see what I felt for you. Apparently, everybody knew."

Sophie said nothing.

"Sophie?"

"Yes?"

"The vow," he whispered.

Alex felt Sophie stiffen, brace herself for something.

"Yes," she said.

"I think I made it so I would wait for you."

Sophie turned to look at him.

"And Sophie," he said.

"Yes?"

"I'm in love with you."

She trembled.

"I love you," he said a little bit louder. "I love you."

Alex grabbed her chin, pulled her face towards his, brushed his lips to hers, teasing, soft then more firm, forced her mouth to open.

"Let me in," he said, deepened the kiss as if his life, his future, his everything depended on this kiss, because it did. He felt her open, respond like she did every time he touched her. He sensed her hesitation, her desire to escape.

"No more running away from me, Sophie. No more."

He refused to let her go. No way she was ever leaving him again. He deepened the kiss, left them both breathless.

"I love you, Sophie Alexander. I need you. I want you. I want you every minute of the day. I don't ever want to be away from you. Sunrise, sunset, together."

What do you want?
The whisper soft in my ear
I want you to find me
I want you here

Epilogue

Sophie

Back in Oregon, Sophie opened her eyes, in her bed, in her cottage, an arm draped around her naked waist, warm, loving. Alex. He stayed the night. He stayed every night now. Always.

Sophie touched his hand, smelled his skin.

"Morning beautiful," groggy, Alex pulled her closer, nuzzled her neck.

Sophie turned, smiled into a pair of sleepy, hungry eyes. Hungry for her.

"I love you," she said.

He smiled, lowered his mouth to hers.

Thank you, Douglas Fairbanks, Sophie thought, *for making my dreams come true.*

Alex

He never thought he could be this happy. This in love. Again. But here she was, her back, legs, hips molded to the front of his naked body. Skin on skin. Heart on heart. Soul on soul. Sophie slept, soft snore escaped her throat, lulled him to peace, to calm. Better than anything, this love which engulfed him from the tip of his big toe, to the top of his head. In his heart. He pulled her closer, vowed never to let her go. Another vow. This one for the living. This one for him. Only for him. He could not breathe without her.

She stirred, soft, "I love you," half asleep. Those three words rocked his world. He kissed her head, tickled her ear with his words. "I love you more." Sleepy eyes turned to him, he lowered his mouth to hers.

Alex could not believe his fortune. He was one lucky bastard.

THE END

Acknowledgements

Thank you to all my peeps, who read, and re-read Sophie, without ever complaining when I asked. Gave me feedback, honed my story, caught my typos, and there were many, encouraged me to go on. I am truly blessed to have so many wonderful people on my side. Unconditional people. Loving people.

Sophie Alexander is a story about romantic love, about hope.

Lucky, that's what I am because I have lived a life surrounded by love.

Thank you, Edgar Bennett, always my cheerleader, an excellent editor and best friend.

Thank you, Carol Lefko, my friend, always happy to read anything I send and provide excellent feedback.

Thank you Julieta Jarquin, for always letting me read out loud to you, for enjoying my stories, never complaining, and asking to hear more.

Gracias Rejas, for keeping all of the stories I wrote as a teenager and young adult. For being my friend since we were born and lived next to each other. For still being my friend.

Thank you, Jobi. Always there for me.

Thank you, Diego, godson extraordinaire, for your invaluable feedback that forced me to dig in, expand, probably not enough for you, but enough for the nature of this story.

Thank you, Gabriela López de Dennis, for, again, formatting my book and helping me with the upload. I am forever technologically challenged, forever grateful for your friendship.

Thank you, Patty Fernandez, for my beautiful website. Exchanged dinners and crochet lessons for the website. I sure got the best end of the deal.

Thank you, Lex Passaris. What can I say to your generous gift of taking my author's picture, for assembling the image that ended up on the cover? You are one talented photographer, generous to a fault. Not an even exchange. Your beautiful work in exchange for cookies. I got the better end of the deal.

Thank you Rebecca Blum, Ellen Deutsch, Ren Bell, for reading the first 10,000 words.

Thank you to my family, all of you, for having my back and loving me.

And thank you Barbara, soul sister, aka Lu, you were the first to read my initial pages, to encourage me, to support me, to inspire me. Always.

Made in the USA
Las Vegas, NV
13 April 2023

70556334R00184